MW01256185

THE MURDER OF THE SAUGATUCK YARN HOARDER

A Saugatuck Murder Mystery

by

G Corwin Stoppel

❖

Lord Hiltensweiller Press

THE SAUGATUCK MURDER MYSTERY SERIES

The Great Saugatuck Murder Mystery

Death by Palette Knife

A Murder of Crows

The Murder of the Saugatuck Yarn Hoarder

ISBN-13: 978-1727832020

ISBN-10: 1727832027

In deepest appreciation of my long time friends,
Rabbi and Ruth Marx —
Scholars, humanitarians, and wonderful friends

Many thanks to Maggie Baker Conklin, ND, who first pitched the idea of a mystery with a yarn hoarder. I'd never heard of yarn hoarding, but she explained that there are many knitters who simply cannot resist buying yet another skein, or two or more, of yarn. In time, they become hoarders. With a flash of a smile she teased, "Dare you." Dare taken; book written; thank-you given.

I am also deeply indebted to my wonderful friends who own numerous red pens, Peter Schakel and John Thomas, and Carson Wilson who corrected a myriad of mistakes and typos, and misspellings galore.

Nor would this book be in your hands right now if it were not for Sally Winthers who produced it. I have never met anyone who is so capable of gently saying 'no' to so many less than stellar ideas. The frustratingly but wonderful thing is that she's usually right!

Above all, to my wife Pat Dewey, who suffered through the clatter of the keyboard, buoyed my spirits, and was constantly encouraging.

FORWARD

This is the fourth book in what has become the Saugatuck Murder Mystery Series. If you have not yet read *The Great Saugatuck Murder Mystery, Death by Palette Knife* and *A Murder of Crows* you might enjoy them. Many of the major characters were introduced in the first one; others came in the second. Like the other books, this story is set in Saugatuck, Michigan in the 1920s.

And, like the previous mysteries, this story is a absolute fiction, but don't let that stop you from enjoying it! The characters are complete works of fiction, and if you think otherwise, you are sadly mistaken. If you even think that there is some resemblance to a real person, living or dead, that is your imagination working over time.

— Fall 2018
   G Corwin Stoppel

THE MURDER OF THE SAUGATUCK YARN HOARDER

CHAPTER ONE

The cold rain that had swept over Saugatuck the two previous days had blown out over night, and to everyone's delight, Decoration Day dawned bright, cloudless, and comfortably warm. Those who were planning on marching in the parade were relieved they would not be soaked, or worse, have their parade cancelled. The spectators anticipated being part of a good crowd along the route to Riverside Cemetery and back, and then convening at the park in the center of town for the formal observance and ceremony. It was the sort of day, decades later, that would put a smile on Owen Smith's face. The long-serving Commander of the local American Legion would tell the marchers, and then the audience, "It never rains on our parade." He was right – usually.

Saugatuck's Decoration Day traditions had been established decades earlier, perhaps in the early 1870's, and only incrementally varied thereafter. Even though the parade would not start until nine o'clock, members of the American Legion and Auxiliary generally began gathering an hour earlier in the upstairs hall at Koening's Hardware store, then spilled out onto the street to join the high school band and other marchers. A little before the hour, two or three open touring cars of veterans from the Civil War slowly pulled up to the corner. Only a few years earlier these men had marched in the parade; now only Mr. Kimsey, decades earlier a drummer boy for one of the Union regiments, still marched, his advanced age giving him the right to lead the procession. Mr. Lincoln's soldiers had passed the torch to the Doughboys who, only a few years earlier, had been in the trenches in France.

At five minutes to the hour the Commander signalled Mr. Kimsey to beat out a long tattoo on his drum, calling the marchers to order. They fell in, snapped to attention, and, on command, stood at ease. Mr. Kimsey marched to the front, with the color guard moving into position behind him, all of them following behind Chief Garrison in his squad car. The Commander and the speaker of the day marched exactly three paces behind. The high school band came next, with the Civil War veterans behind them, and bringing up the rear were the young men from the Great War. Trailing discreetly behind was the fire brigade with their new truck and the old two-wheeled hose cart pulled by some young men.

If the parade was anchored by upholding old tradition, so also were the spectators. Those along the route would wait for the parade to come past their house and at the last minute hurry out the front door to stand in silent tribute. A few men saluted, as did the majority of young boys. Once the fire trucks went down the street, many of them would walk to the park. Others, not living along the route, would go straight to the park and wait for the parade to arrive. Most years, like the neighbors on their block, Phoebe and her mother Harriet did not hurry down to Koening's to see the start of the parade. They let it come to them, then walked to the park.

This year was different. They broke their tradition and walked several blocks to Koening's, and for good reason. Phoebe's grandfather, Doctor Horace Balfour, was going to be the speaker. "We have to be ten minutes early or we're going to be late," the girl had urged her mother, tugging her along the sidewalk. "That's what Grandfather always says."

Even from half a block away, she instantly spotted her grandfather standing with the other veterans and a sprinkling of civilians who had come up to him. As always, he was ramrod straight, tall, thin, an aura of almost imperial dignity surrounding him, his once brown hair now silver. In Phoebe's eyes he looked more handsome than ever in his uniform. Nor was she the only woman who felt that way. Harriet smiled when she saw some of her women friends look at him approvingly, or flash a quick smile his direction. Phoebe picked up her pace, pulling her mother along behind her, as she hurried down the sidewalk to get close so she could wish him well with his address.

For both mother and daughter, each for her own reasons, the only cloud that morning was not in the sky, but in the form of Doctor Beatrix Howell. Harriet had come to know her at Ox-Bow when Beatrix first came a few summers earlier to paint. The two women, despite the difference in age, had a congenial relationship, but certainly not a close one, that was now beginning to ice over. Harriet had found Beatrix too austere, too formal and literal when she spoke, and distant and disengaged from everyone around her. For her part, Beatrix was never at ease except in very formal settings. By the 1920s, Ox-Bow, like Saugatuck itself, had acquired a collection of mildly eccentric people, and for those who met her, it was a matter of Beatrix being Beatrix. Still, there were times when Harriet thought the woman went beyond eccentric to spooky.

The real problem, and a constant and growing worry, was that Beatrix and Horace had seemingly grown closer to each other. They had been childhood friends who, after graduation from high school, had drifted apart for decades. Two summers earlier they had accidently reconnected in Saugatuck. At first, Harriet was happy her father-in-law had a friend outside of his own family and a few colleagues at his hospital. It took some of the pressure off her, because Horace was sometimes gruff, impatient, and imperious. Worse, he was painfully lonely, and sometimes Harriet felt obligated to look after him. He needed a friend, but her attitude toward Beatrix began to change when it looked like their relationship might become something more than collegial. She could not quite discern its nature, and feared where it might lead. More than once she had told herself, "I'm probably worrying about nothing, and just borrowing trouble." Still, she continued to worry.

Phoebe saw Beatrix as a potential rival for her grandfather's affection, a woman who had the potential to steal him away from her. She admired the woman's brainpower and was amused by her sometimes stilted old-fashioned way of talking. She envied Beatrix flying her own airplane and being one of the few women in the country, maybe the world, who was a pilot. She delighted watching Beatrix casually taking her grandfather's pipe and puffing on it, or lighting up a cigar. No other woman in Saugatuck was that brazen, and if for no other reason than it irritated her mother, Phoebe liked it. If Beatrix hadn't become her rival, they might have become very good friends. As far as Phoebe was concerned, when her grandfather came to Saugatuck, she had exclusive rights to his time and companionship. Beatrix was in the way. One morning on the way to school, when Janie Bird asked her about her grandfather's friend, Phoebe asked, "You mean the woman who walks like this?" and imitated her stiff gait and her arms rigidly at her side. Jane had laughed, and immediately Phoebe regretted being so nasty and childish.

Even though they never said it, much less discussed it between themselves, both mother and daughter realized that rejecting Beatrix would only threaten their own sometimes-fragile relationship with Horace. Reject or snub her, and he would be hurt and retreat all the more into himself. Or worse, it might drive them closer to each other.

It was bad enough that the previous autumn Horace and Beatrix had each decided on their own to come to Saugatuck to sort out the mystery of the three dead crows. Phoebe blamed herself for that blunder because she had written to both of them. Now, the two of them were back in town, having intentionally planned to travel together.

Just as they were walking up to Horace, Beatrix intercepted them. "Harriet, I just saw the most unusual woman, and I hope you will say that she is not a permanent resident. Just minutes ago she was telling Chief Garrison not to drive so fast this year because it was not appropriate to look like he was hurrying the parade along. She finished with him and the next minute ordered the commander to make sure the men were marching in step! Now it appears she is about to begin instructing Horace on how to give a speech. She is a most unusual woman. By any chance do you know her name?" She pointed to a thin, elderly woman with long blondish-gray hair.

"Fairy Nightshade," Phoebe blurted out, then instantly clapped her hand over her mouth in horror. It was one thing for adult women to use that nickname behind the woman's back, but her mother had forbidden her to do it. She had done it once before, only to be met by Harriet's fierce glare at her breach of etiquette. "That isn't nice. Her name is Miss Nason. You must respect your elders. I don't want to hear you talk about her that way ever again, is that clear?" For a moment Phoebe had considered asking why it was perfectly acceptable for older women to call her by that nasty nickname, but not acceptable for her. Then she thought better of it. Parents and teachers called it "talking back," even when their children were merely asking for information.

Harriet turned to Beatrix. "That's Miss Phyllis Nason," she said, looking over her glasses at Beatrix. "She's not someone that is, well, always congenial, nor well-liked. Let's just say most of us find it easier to keep our distance. The more distance, the better, to be truthful. She is, well, just too instructional for most of us. She constantly instructs everyone what to do.

"Phoebe, dear, be a real sweetheart and go rescue your grandfather from, well, you know who. Just go over and let him know how handsome he looks in his uniform. As soon as the parade starts I want you to join us at our usual spot in the park. Do you understand, dear?" She watched as her daughter hurried over to greet her grandfather. Horace did the expected. He turned away from Fairy Nightshade and focused on Phoebe.

As soon as Phoebe was talking with her grandfather, Harriet said, "Let's go claim our spot before it's taken, shall we? We'll wait for the parade to return."

"Yes, thank you. Am I to understand you are trying to avoid the woman?" Beatrix asked.

"Yes. Life is easier without an encounter with Fairy Nightshade, especially on a beautiful morning. We all try to avoid her as much as we can," she answered as she caught Phoebe's attention and pointed in the general direction of a huge ancient elm, then ambled to her favorite spot.

From a distance they could hear the parade returning into town, and like the others, they craned their necks and looked down the street just as Chief Garrison's car made the corner and turned onto Water Street. A few younger boys who had raced over to the chain ferry landing to collect the spent shells from the rifle salute to those who died at sea came running back. They knew where the honor guard would stand in the park and wanted to get in position to collect more trophies. "Isn't it a perfect morning for Decoration Day?" Harriet asked, hoping to draw Beatrix out. "Blue sky, not too hot, not too cold, and not too much wind for the men carrying the flags, either. No wonder so many people turned out for it."

"Yes, yes it is a very seasonal morning," Beatrix said distantly.

"Even Fairy Nightshade can't spoil it," Harriet answered, thankful Phoebe had not yet joined them and heard her use the forbidden nickname.

The police chief slowly drove past the crowd waiting in the park on Butler, shamelessly waving to people on the left side of the street as if he were a political candidate. With dignity and respect for the solemnity of the day, the marchers kept their eyes straight forward, oblivious to the cheers and applause from the spectators.

The dignified respect for the war dead was marred only by the distraction of Fairy Nightshade, who was furiously pedalling her bicycle full speed as she raced up the street. Anyone who knew her, or knew of her reputation, wondered where she was going. A few joked that she wanted to get to the podium first, hoping to claim it for herself, but she kept going. A man on the sidewalk in front of Harriet and Beatrix joked, "I'll bet it would be a crackerjack of a speech, too." The others standing nearby laughed. One of them said, "Probably she's gone out to Riverside to make sure the dead are still lying at attention."

Harriet ignored them, quickly changing the subject. "When Phoebe was much younger, I always used this parade as a way of teaching American history," Harriet told Beatrix, trying to change the conversation. "I pointed out the soldiers from the Civil War, and how they had freed the slaves. And for a year or two there was a man who had been with Admiral Dewey in Manila, so I told her about the Spanish American War, and the Great War after that. I think it helped make a connection to see men who had been there with what she read in her textbooks."

"Yes, she would experience living history. You truly are a very good mother." Beatrix said, her eyes following Horace as he marched beyond them.

Harriet spotted Phoebe coming towards them. "And, just where have you been young lady? No, wait! Let me guess. Your friend Henry is in the band..."

Phoebe rewarded her mother with a blush. "I was walking with Grandfather, but on the sidewalk, not in the parade!"

"It may seem quite odd coming from me, but I find there is nothing quite so handsome as a man in uniform," Beatrix said over the percussion section of the band marching in front of them. Both mother and daughter stiffened at her comment. It was unusually bold for her.

"Especially if it is Grandfather or Uncle Theo." Phoebe froze at her own words and instantly changed the subject. "Did you fly here in your aeroplane?

"Yes," she answered in her flat voice. "Perhaps if your mother will give you permission, you can go up with me sometime."

Phoebe pretended not to hear, and didn't answer, focusing on the mayor and several members of the Village Council who were glad-handing the crowds.

The three women were joined by the crowd who flooded off the sidewalks into the street to follow behind the fire truck to the park. It took a few minutes for the band and the honor guard to get into position, and for some of "Mr Lincoln's Ready Made Soldiers," as they sometimes called themselves, to slowly make their way to the waiting chairs. Finally, the commander stepped up to a megaphone mounted on a tripod, holding up his hands to get the crowd's attention. "Folks, if you'll settle down, we're about to get started!" Gradually the crowd quieted. While he waited to start the ceremony, he noticed a man jogging up to Chief Garrison, panting hard, and telling him something that indicated a sense of urgency. The chief jumped back into his car, and with the siren wailing, roared up Butler Street. Everyone watched, asking others near them what was happening, and wondering where he was going.

The same man ran to the men in the Fire Brigade to give them a message. They looked at each other, confused as everyone else, then quickly decided that they should follow the police chief. They clamored onto their trucks, and with bells clanging and horns blaring, they parted the crowd like Moses at the Red Sea and picked up speed once they got past Koening's Hardware store. Three members of the color guard, volunteer firemen, handed off their flags to other veterans and joined in the dash after their chief and the fire brigade.

"What the blazes is going on?" the commander growled. "We're here to honor the War Dead!"

From somewhere at the edge of the crowd a man shouted. "House fire up on the hill!"

"Up on the hill" was not a very satisfactory explanation. It was more alarming than anything else. Half the town lived in that area, and all of them immediately worried that it might be their house. They ran after the police and fire brigade. Others decided to follow them, and in less than a minute, the park was emptying out.

CHAPTER TWO

"It was sheer herd mentality, lemmings rushing off to find the nearest cliff," Beatrix would tell Clarice later that day. "Pandemonium. No decorum, no sense of order."

The commander looked around, hands on hips in utter frustration, uncertain what to do. Weeks of work and preparation were being ruined as the ceremony unravelled. Phoebe watched it all, and a wicked thought crossed her mind and put a smile on her face. "Too bad Fairy Nightshade isn't here to tell people what to do."

Suddenly the commander wheeled around to face the color guard, calling them to order. "We will still honor the war dead!" he bellowed. "Sergeant at Arms, you will place the wreath." He waited until a small wreath of poppies was put in place, then shouted, "Salute the dead!" The soldiers snapped to attention, the volley of shots was fired, and a trumpeter played "Taps."

The commander looked at the veterans and the band, turned to look at the small crowd, and snarled, "Dismissed!" The park was nearly deserted except for a handful of people milling around.

That was the end of it. Decoration Day, or at least the formal part of it, was over. The honor guard had been dismissed, some spectators helped the old soldiers back into the cars, and the commander walked over to Doctor Horace. "Real sorry about the way this turned out, General. I sure didn't see this happening. We usually have a good tribute. I'm just sorry it happened the year when you are here. Maybe we can prevail upon you to return next year?" he asked.

The old surgeon told him it was quite all right, trying to make light of it. "If I hadn't been asked to give the speech, I might have gone off to see the fire myself. Those folks were right. A fire is a lot more exciting than listening to some old codger telling them what they already know."

"Say, you got it written out, your speech, I mean? Why don't you let me see if my buddy over to the newspaper will print it? That way at least folks could read it." Doctor Horace was a bit hesitant, but handed the carefully typed pages to the commander.

"Well, folks, that was unexpected," Horace repeated to his family, forcing a grim smile. "What say we go back to the hotel and have a late breakfast or early lunch? My treat." Before they could answer he started walking south along Butler street, trusting the others would follow.

"It is a pity about your speech, Horace," Beatrix said, catching up with him and falling in step.

"Well, it might be a blessing in disguise," he told her. "You never know. It could have been a real dud. That's happened to me before."

Phoebe's eyes squinted in dismay when she heard her rival answer, "Yes, perhaps." Even if Beatrix were correct, which Phoebe absolutely and positively knew she was not, it wasn't a very nice thing to say. The woman had agreed with her grandfather when she should have disagreed.

"It is too bad Fred isn't here today. He'd have loved the parade and then the fire," Harriet said a bit too brightly, trying to change the subject.

"Thunderation! He'd be rescuing cats, catching babies tossed out of a burning house, and we'd never hear the end of it."

"Well, at least it'll be a change from hearing how he single-handedly won the war, saved General Pershing's life, and turned back

Hindenburg all on his own," Phoebe giggled. Her mother looked over the top of her glasses at her, irritated at her lack of respect, even if she was trying to lighten the mood.

"You're right about that, Phoebe," Horace said, rescuing her. "We'll take small blessings where we can find them."

Their timing at the hotel was not the best. Breakfast was over and the dining room was empty. The hostess explained they had such a small breakfast crowd because of the parade and ceremony that they closed early. "Lunch will start in half an hour."

"At your convenience," Horace said quietly. "We're the ones who interrupted your plans. It's a nice morning. We'll be out on the front porch. Let us know when you're ready, would you please?" They had been sitting for only a few minutes when a car sped down the street in their direction and came to a hard stop in front of them. "Thunderation! This can't be good news," Horace muttered.

"Looks like that to me, too! Something's up, and I'll bet it has to do with the fire," Phoebe said.

A boy she knew from high school, a senior who worked as a soda jerk at Parrish's drugstore, jumped out of the car and came bounding up the stairs. "Chief Garrison says for you to come on the double-quick," he panted.

"For a fire?" Horace asked, squinting at him. "Thunderation, man! We're about to have brunch."

"It's more than your run of the mill fire. The firemen got it put out fast, but there's a dead body in there. The chief told me to tell you to pretend you're a caisson and get rolling. He said to tell you to bring along your doctor bag, too. 'Bring along your doctor bag,' that's what he said. Car's waiting for you, Doctor Balfour. So's the chief."

"Slow down. Doctor Landis is the medical examiner, not me."

"I know that, sir, but he and his boy went up the Kalamazoo to the dam at Allegan to fish. That's why the chief wants you. Now, Sir!"

Doctor Horace nodded in acknowledgement, and turned to Phoebe asking her to run up to his room and get his bag. While he waited for her, he turned around and asked Beatrix, "You want in on this?"

She froze. She had absolutely no interest in any new adventure that involved Chief Garrison and a death. Then again, she had no desire to stay on the porch with Harriet and Phoebe, and probably lunch with just the two of them if he was delayed at the scene. Going on a medical call with Horace and another encounter with the police chief seemed the lesser of two evils. Her lips were tight as she said, "One last time. Into the breach, once again."

"I'm Axel. Axel Jensen," the young man said, reaching out to shake hands with the two physicians. "I'll fill you in on the details on the way there. Well, I can tell you now, I guess. Older woman, living alone. Her name was Miss Nason, and she used to be a substitute teacher. I never had her for a sub, but that's what they say. The fire was in the kitchen, but they found her dead on the floor of a closet in the back of the house."

"Was the door opened or closed?" Beatrix asked. "And was it the first floor?"

"Yes, to both of your questions, Miss. Closed. Least that's what I think the fire captain told the chief. I'm pretty sure of it. I didn't see it myself. Yeah, that's what he said. The door was closed on account of the fact the firemen had to open it to get to her."

Beatrix smiled and she was energized again. "Now, that does makes it much more interesting. I will come with you."

"What was the deceased's name, again, please?" Horace asked.

"I think the chief said it was a Miss Nason. Yeah, that's right. Nason," the young man repeated.

"That is the woman I saw earlier," Beatrix said flatly. "How tragic."

"It certainly is," Harriet answered quietly, her head down.

Phoebe was confused. Her mother, like most of the adult women, despised Miss Nason, calling her Fairy Nightshade behind her back. Like nearly everyone else, they avoided her whenever they could, yet when they did have to talk with her, they were polite, as if she were a very good friend. She couldn't understand why her mother was so upset that Miss Nason was dead. Adults could be strange like that, and Phoebe thought that in some ways it wasn't being honest.

It took only a few minutes to get to the Nason house. The fire had already been extinguished, but the fire brigade stood around, hoses at the ready, in case a hot spot should break out again. "Really sorry about interrupting your speech like this, General," one of the younger men said. "I was looking forward to hearing it. My brother was over in France at Belleau Woods with the Marines."

"And I was looking forward to delivering it," Doctor Horace smiled. It surprised him that the fireman knew his rank, until he realized he was still in his old uniform. "Belleau Woods? Those boys had a rough time of it. But they stuck it out and won. That's what counts!"

"Well, if you want to do it now, we've got to hang around a while longer."

"Thank you for the offer, but I'll hold onto it for now. Maybe I'll get invited back some year and can use it then. You won't want to hear it twice, and if you don't remember it, I'd be hurt. Right now, I've got some business to attend to."

Several of the fireman saluted him, and to their joy, Doctor Horace pulled himself to attention and returned their salute.

Chief Garrison came out of the house and spotted the doctors. He ambled over to where they were standing by the curb. "Well, I didn't need both of you," he snapped. "One would have done. Is she or isn't she dead? That's the question, and it doesn't take two of you to figure that out. That's what I need to know, and if she is, I need you to certify she is a goner." He was as brusque as ever, not having the decency to say hello, much less to apologize for interrupting their plans when he summoned them.

"Always a delight to see you, too," Horace said with a touch of sarcasm in his voice.

"The deceased is through here. We left her right where we found her," the chief continued. "Follow me."

Horace and Beatrix hurried to keep up with the chief as he led them across the lawn. Whether by design or for some other reason, once they stepped into the house Beatrix stopped to methodically look at everything in the room. Eventually, she followed behind them, slowly and silently inspecting everything.

The acrid smoke that clung in the air of the house made Horace's eyes burn and water. The chief led them down a short hallway, hurrying them past the other rooms. "Fire was contained in the kitchen. We found her in this big storage room. Looks to me like she tried to hide in here or rescue something, got over-come, and pulled that big set of shelves down on top of herself."

They looked at the room, dumbstruck by the contents. "Thunderation! That woman had enough yarn to start a business," Horace snarled. "Look at the stuff. Yarn, material. It's everywhere!"

"Who moved the shelves?" Beatrix asked when she eventually joined the two men. She slowly surveyed the room, looking at two large shelving units stacked with skeins of yarn, one that had toppled to the floor, the other still against the opposite wall, plus a table with several boxes of yarn on top and underneath. She slowly surveyed the room, her face expressionless.

"The firemen. They saw her legs sticking out from this end, and thought maybe she was trapped alive. I guess, well, no guess about it, they were a bit too late. Well, you two get on with the examination and see if she's dead or not. If she is, then I've got to send some-one down to the furniture store to bring up the hearse."

The two doctors knelt beside the late Miss Nason, did a routine examination, and both nodded in agreement that she was indeed dead. Horace put his stethoscope back into his black bag. "Deceased."

"Well, that's what I thought, too, but I thought we ought to be sure. So, that's that," the chief said. He let out a low whistle. "This'll be a real loss to the community. She was one of those society women types who helped out all the time with everything. A real loss. Smart, too. She was a teacher, in case you didn't already know it. Well, thank you for your help. I'll let you get back to whatever you were doing. Axel can drive you back to the hotel and then get some-one to bring up the hearse."

"If you don't mind me saying so, we pronounced her dead. We didn't say anything about a cause of death," Horace reminded him.

"Looks pretty obvious to me. She was overcome by the smoke and when she collapsed, she pulled those shelves down on top of herself," the chief said sharply.

"Maybe, or maybe not, and that's something you'll find out with a postmortem."

"Now, look here you two. Every time I ask you to do a simple little medical job you make it into a big deal. That fellow out to Ox-Bow was a nice simple robbery and murder until you stuck your noses into it and made a mess of things. And then last fall you came up with some cock-a-mamie story about poison plants and dead French painters, and I had the murderer already locked up in the jail...."

Beatrix interrupted. "Dutch. He was a Dutch painter."

The chief glared at her. "I don't care and it doesn't matter. French, Dutch, a Hottentot for all the difference it makes to me."

"He was Dutch. I understand your sentiments, and yet as you are undoubtedly aware, we were right both times," Beatrix shot back at him.

"All I'm saying is that you will need a determination of a cause of death for the certificate. There is nothing to get excited about," Horace said with a surprisingly calm voice. "As you said, we're finished here, and we're going on our way. If you need us, you know where we're staying. Then, as soon as the Aurora arrives we'll be on the boat."

When they walked back outside, Axel was waiting near the squad car, offering a ride. Beatrix declined, telling him that they would enjoy the morning walk. A block away from Miss Nason's home, when she was certain no one was around, she stopped suddenly and turned to face Horace. "She did not die of natural causes. I believe she was murdered."

Horace's concentration was interrupted. Far away he heard a low, deep boom. A smile crept across his face. With a bit of luck it was the signal cannon from the Aurora and that meant that his brother Theo and Theo's wife Clarice would soon be arriving. And with them, Fred and his car and the Garwoods.

"Horace," Beatrix repeated. "She did not die of natural causes."

CHAPTER THREE

"Murdered? Beatrix, how are you so sure of that?" Horace asked.

"We will sit down at a park bench and I will explain my reasons" she replied. "Then we can dissect and discuss it." They walked in silence down Griffith Street, and turned right on Main and went to the park across the street where they found two vacant benches, facing each other. Beatrix flashed a quick smile. She was more comfortable facing Horace than sitting next to him.

"All right," Horace said, "start at the beginning."

Beatrix stared straight ahead for a full minute, still silently marshalling her thoughts. "Just before the ceremony started, we saw Miss Nason practically flying down the street on her bicycle. I overheard a number of people speak disparagingly of her, but thought nothing more about it. In a small town, there is an abundance of gossip, often very dismissive of an individual with a unique personality, so that is not unusual in and of itself. She missed the parade and what would have been the ceremony. Considering what I have observed and heard from others, her absence must have been highly unusual."

Horace held up a hand to stop her. "Perhaps she remembered she left the gas burning on the stove, or couldn't remember whether it was on or off, or something like that. By the time she got there, there was a fire. Then she panicked and went into that storage room. Children do it all the time, with usually the same results. They try hiding instead of getting out of the house. The results are usually tragic. Or, perhaps she was trying to save something valuable."

"Granted," Beatrix said. "It is tragic, and I agree it is an all too common mistake in judgement. We must also keep in mind that the chief wanted us to pronounce her dead. I saw how he rushed you through the house. Then, we were rushed to perform a very brief examination, and each of us individually came to the same conclusion. She was already dead. A first-year medical student would have come to the same conclusion. Upon that point we agree. After that, the chief's words and behavior made it very clear that our presence was no longer welcome. When you reminded him of a postmortem, he became enraged and was barely able to control himself. I observed how his fists were clenching and unclenching, and his heart rate increased enough to make the small veins in his cheeks more pronounced. Even his voice was pitched slightly higher."

"Slow down, Beatrix. We aren't his favorite people, and we have a long unpleasant history with him," Horace reminded her.

"And, he with us, I agree. This is not a mutual admiration society, which is of little importance right now. I do not believe he is a well educated man, and certainly unaware of how to deal with the public. He is a hothead and not very sophisticated. There is nothing I find admirable about him. I do not like him, and I do not approve of his methods. We must look beyond that because something is not right. I find all of this very curious," she said. She leaned closer and barely whispered, "Particularly, that bruise on the left side of Miss Nason's head that extends from the temple back past the ear."

"That could have been where she got hit when that yarn rack, or whatever you want to call it, came down on her," he answered. "That's what Doctor Landis will have to decide at the autopsy."

"You may be right. That might be all that did happen. A fire, smoke, and an accident. I am not convinced it was that simple, and I do not believe we are able to make a determination without further examination," she answered.

They sat in silence, each of them thinking, until finally Horace said quietly, "Then I think we need an invitation to the post-mortem."

"An invitation? And how do you think the chief is going to feel about that?" Beatrix asked him.

"He'll bust his garters!" Horace laughed. "Now, if Fred were sitting here he'd say we need to out-flank him, just the way he did when he was fighting Kaiser Bill!"

Beatrix looked at him with disdain. "Are Fred's comments relevant? Horace, please stay focused. You are taking the royal jelly I gave you, I assume. You seem somewhat addled."

"The chief wants nothing to do with us, and Landis can be a bit prickly at times, so he might not want us underfoot. So, yes, Fred's method might work," he told her seriously. "And yes, I am taking the royal jelly."

"I see. You have a point. Do you have a plan?"

"Now, if you were a newspaperman, just where would you be, considering it's Decoration Day?" Horace asked.

"I would probably be out fishing, sailing, or playing golf, perhaps having a picnic with my family. But considering how this Decoration Day was spoiled, I would probably be at my typewriter working hard on a story to be on the front page above the fold."

"Exactly," Horace said. "Well done, Irene." She responded with a thin smile. He glanced in the direction of the Maplewood Hotel and smiled. "We'll save some shoe leather if we call first to make sure the editor is in."

"I do not understand what you mean," she said.

"We'll call from there to see if he is at the office. Better that than walking over there on a fool's errand."

"Oh, I see! Yes, that makes very good sense," Beatrix answered. "I will wait here for you and enjoy the quiet morning and think more about this incident."

Horace was away for a few minutes, and when he returned, he had an amused look on his face. "Looks like we got skunked. It wasn't just Doctor Landis and his son who went fishing. The editor and his boys went, too."

"Perhaps it is just as well. I believe there may be a squall moving in. While you were at the hotel I heard more rumbles of thunder," Beatrix said.

"I doubt it," Horace replied, looking up at the Carolina blue sky. "It's Fred playing with the cannon to let us know they'll be here anytime. And my guess is that Theo is having fun with it, too." He held out his hand to help her off the bench, but she ignored the gesture, stood and continued walking with him.

"Horace, we must talk. You have been very gracious inviting me to stay on your boat, but are you sure that is wise? I do not believe that Harriet and Phoebe are comfortable with the idea, or with me even being in Saugatuck. I also know that you have been teased by Theo because of me. Perhaps I should stay at the Butler Hotel or the Colonial. I could see if there is a vacancy at the Maplewood. I would not be offended if you would be more comfortable that way."

They paused in front of the Post Office. "I've had a lifetime of teasing from Theo, and I know how to handle it and him. As for the others, well, it seems to me the last time we were here you said women are sometimes each others' worst enemies. They're just jealous, that's all. Let 'em fuss. That's what I say: Let 'em fuss."

"What about Harriet and Phoebe? I do not want to be a cause of disquiet between you and your family. I am very firm about that."

"I understand, and I'm grateful. It's more kind of you than you realize. You won't cause problems."

"You are quite certain?" she asked softly.

"Quite certain. Give them a little while, and they'll come around. So, pack your bags, get your skates on, and let's board the ship once they get her tied off. The bellhop will have them sent over once we leave."

"Shouldn't we have lunch with Harriet and Phoebe? We promised, remember?" she asked. "And, Horace, why would I wear skates at this time of the year?"

"It's just an expression. It means to get moving. As for the girls, I doubt they waited for us. You realize we've been gone a couple of hours?" Horace asked, putting his watch back in his pocket. He heard Beatrix breathe a sigh of relief.

"You know, I've never watched the Aurora come into port. I've always been on her when we tie up," Horace shouted up to his brother who was leaning on the rail, watching three men pull on the ropes to tie it into place along the docks. "My compliments to the captain."

"Looks like you're waiting, bag and baggage!" Theo teased.

"I am, and it's not for the Robert E. Lee, either." He watched as several men finished their work and signalled that the ship was tied up. "You mind getting the gangplank lowered? This summer! Thunderation, I'm in the waiting room," he teased.

"Well, you got something worth waiting for once you do get aboard!" Theo called down. "You're in for a surprise. Bet you'll never guess who we've got on the ship."

"What in thunderation are you two doing here? And how did you get on?" Horace laughed as he stood on the deck..

"Well, Grandfather, we were sitting on the porch and we heard the signal cannon when it was way out on the lake. When you and Doctor Howell didn't come back for lunch, we drove to Ox-Bow and then walked out to the breakwater. Captain Garwood saw us and picked us up. We wanted to surprise you," Phoebe said.

"Well, how do you like that? You pulled a pretty good one on me!" Horace cheered. After greeting Captain and Mrs. Garwood, Fred, and Theo and Clarice, he announced that he was going down to his cabin and change out of his uniform. "Never realized wool could get this hot. Fred and Theo, give me a few minutes and then join me in the library. You, too, Beatrix."

"Grandfather!" Phoebe wailed as she came across the deck and paused in front of his library door. "You've repaired the Aurora!"

"What do you mean?" Horace asked.

"What happened to the bullet holes? They're gone. I thought you told me they were trophies!" She was near tears.

"Oh, I wouldn't worry, Phoebs. Knowing your grandfather, he's sure to acquire some new ones before the end of the summer," Theo consoled her.

"I should hope not!" Harriet replied. Beatrix's face blanched at the thought of it. Horace just winked at Phoebe and then ran his right finger across the side of his nose. She winked back and, for the moment, all seemed well.

"Harriet told us the latest," Theo said, sliding into one of the leather chairs. "Someone didn't want to listen to you yammering at the ceremony so they set their house on fire and got killed in the deal."

"I do not believe Horace was the cause of it," Beatrix said quickly, missing his attempt at humor.

"No. No, of course not," Theo replied. "But a fire and death, none-theless. I'm waiting for one of you to say that you think it was foul play, so let's hear it."

"I believe it was murder," Beatrix said flatly.

Theo looked up at the ceiling. "Not again?" he whined.

"Oh, I don't know. It's a shame someone got killed, but it is rather exciting, don't you think?" Horace asked. He looked over at Beatrix and saw her flash a shy smile.

"Grandfather, there's someone here to see you. It's Doctor Landis." Horace thanked Phoebe, then turned to Beatrix, "I'd say we got our answer. And my guess is that we're getting an invitation to an autopsy."

Phoebe ushered Doctor Landis into her grandfather's library. "I heard you had taken your boy fishing," Horace said as he greeted him. "I'm surprised to see you back so soon."

"Well, that didn't work out so well. My boy got a bit sick to his stomach, so we came home early."

"That's sad to hear. Nothing better than a day fishing with your boys," Theo said, reaching out his hand to greet the physician. "And you remember our colleague, Doctor Howell?"

"Yes, yes, of course. It occurred to me last autumn, just after you had left, that I first saw you when you gave a talk in Pittsburgh about fifteen years ago. I was a first-year resident then. I wish I'd thought to tell you earlier. I never imagined seeing any of you in a small town like Saugatuck, much less working with you. I'm hon-ored. Triple honored!"

"I spoke on new methods of pathology when presented with early stage prostate cancer," Beatrix explained to the Balfour brothers. "It was a two-stage method of taking a biopsy prior to surgery, preparing the tissue for examination by flash freezing it in an iodine solution, and making a determination as to surgery then or later. Now, it seems rather primitive and slow. Alas, soon afterward Doctor McCarthy of Edinburgh developed a much faster method of doing a biopsy while the patient was already prepped and in the operating room."

Doctor Landis said, "Yes, I remember that now. Say, I don't want to take up your day, so I'll come straight to the point. I'll be doing the autopsy tomorrow on the Nason case. Can you be there? I would truly be grateful if you were attending. I know you're all on vacation, so you probably don't have your scrubs with you. Not to worry. I seem to be well supplied. Shall we agree to nine o'clock?"

A round of handshakes, and the town doctor left. "And now, maybe we can finally enjoy the rest of the holiday," Theo sighed with relief.

"Before you go, Theo, I want to hear why Beatrix thinks this might be far more complicated than an accidental death," Horace said.

"Her skin color, for one thing," Beatrix replied. We know that she had been riding her bicycle at break-neck speed through town, then two blocks up a moderately steep hill. We must remember that she was an older woman. I suspect she already heard that her house was on fire. She would have been terrified, her pulse racing. When she got there she would have been all the more agitated if she saw smoke. There should have been a blush on her face, and yet it was ashen. We arrived a short time after the event, and she was definitely pale. There are some other possible indicators. But, we must stop with the initial observation so that we do not prejudice our minds tomorrow. That is all I will say on this subject." She turned and left the library for her cabin.

"My guess is that there is a little more to this story; more than she told us just now," Theo said when the two of them were alone.

"There is a slight hematoma on the side of her head. It was not a sufficiently harsh blow to break the skin, but the location is interesting. We'll know more tomorrow morning. You can ask Beatrix then, because she's the one who found it."

The next morning Doctor Landis and his three colleagues, dressed in surgical garb and masks, crowded around the examination table. "I've asked my nurse to be present and take notes," he explained, nodding to a tired, pale middle-aged woman sitting at a nearby desk.

"I have brought along my camera should we need it to document any evidence. I believe we will need it," Beatrix said quietly.

Doctor Landis nodded for her to begin.

"The first thing we observe is that there has been a serious concussion on the left side of the head, just above the ear and below the crown of the head, beginning at the temple and extending to the ear," she told them. "Surprisingly, there were no abrasions or punctures on the skin, and as a result, no visible presenting evidence of blood." She invited Doctor Landis to confirm her observation. He gently ran his finger along Miss Nason's skull, then nodded to the nurse to note it. All of them paused while Beatrix took pictures from several angles. "No fracturing of the skull," Landis added.

"We will return to that later. If she died of smoke inhalation, we will find particles on her nasal hair, lips, mouth, and throat," Beatrix said firmly, as if she was teaching medical students or residents. With swabs in hand, she set to work. "As you can see, there is no indication of particles. However, further examination under a microscope will be essential before we make a final determination. Doctor Landis, would you expose the ribs, please? Horace and Theo, the rib spreader, so we can examine a lung."

While the three prepared for the next step, Beatrix took the four swabs to the nurse, asking her to label and mark them, and carefully set them aside so they would not contaminate each other. She returned to the examination table to wait for the left lung to be exposed.

"Well, in a way, her death might have been fortunate now rather than later. Advanced lung cancer," Doctor Landis quietly announced after he had lifted out the lung. He pointed to the tumor.

"At least it was fast and relatively painless this way," Theo said, looking up sadly. "Not a pleasant way to die – lung cancer. Biopsies?" he asked.

"Definitely, both the cancerous portion of the lower lung and near the top. Again, you will notice there is no discoloration of the lung which normally presents itself in death by smoke inhalation," Beatrix replied. Each small tissue section was carefully put in a Petri dish, labelled, then moved to a refrigerator. While the three surgeons were working, Beatrix's camera was snapping away. "Two frames left," she observed.

"Make 'em count," Horace encouraged her, raising his eyebrows as he smiled beneath his mask.

"Yes, of course. Thank you, Doctor," she said formally. "I had the forethought to bring another two rolls. While we have the chest cavity opened, we will look at her heart for possible myocardial infarction and cardiac arrest. I believe we will rule out that as a possible cause of death. Doctor Theo, I believe this is your area of expertise, so would you do the honors, please?"

They stood by as Theo bent over the patient, carefully examining Miss Nason's heart. "Nothing," he said finally. "Her heart is in perfect condition for a woman decades younger."

All four stood straight, looking at Beatrix for the next step to take. "I believe it would be appropriate to close," she said.

Out of respect, they carefully slipped the lung into the chest cavity, and slowly unscrewed the chest spreader. Theo offered to sew up the incision. "My brother has the most beautiful stitches," Horace explained to Doctor Landis. "If he hadn't become a surgeon he would have made an excellent tailor or milliner," he teased.

Beatrix ignored his jibe and continued her lecture. "Since we did not find any indication, yet – I will add, we now return to the left side of the skull.

"It appears that the blow came from above. That would be the result of the cabinet coming down on top of her, if indeed that is what happened. We cannot discount that she was struck by a person or persons unknown. A sharp blow in that location can easily push the brain down, which often presses against the portion of the brain responsible for breathing, the medulla. As we know, if a normally healthy person chooses to hold his breath, the medulla and pons temporarily cease functioning. When the person gasps for breath, they resume functioning as normal. A blow, or concussion, on the top of the skull, or in this case, near the top, will create the same result. In the deceased's case, she was unconscious and here is the result. She did not resume breathing. Doctors, we can examine further, but I am quite certain I am right. Are there any additional questions, doctors?"

After removing their surgical gear and cleaning up, Theo asked, "So, what do we have?"

"Nothing, really," Horace told him. "The preliminary work gives the appearance Miss Nason didn't die of smoke inhalation or the fire, but even that's not certain. The lab work on the tissue samples will be next."

"Doctor Landis, as the village physician, I believe that responsibility falls to you, as you will be signing the death certificate," Beatrix said flatly. "I believe we should also look much more closely at the bruise on the left side of her head, from the temple to above the ear. It may prove significant. And, of course, the medulla and pons for additional evidence of trauma."

"Or not," Theo muttered. "She got jostled around enough yesterday. The evidence might not be there."

"Yes, yes I figure you're right about that. The thing is, I'm standing here with the nation's foremost forensic pathologist, and I'll be jiggered if I'm going to let that opportunity slip through my fingers," Landis answered. "I want to do some further examination. We may not learn anything about Miss Nason, but I believe I will learn something from working with you, Doctor Howell."

Beatrix looked at him, somewhat confused and not quite understanding what he meant. She glanced at Horace, who barely nodded his head in support of her.

"In that case, I am honoured, and am at your disposal," she said flatly.

"Good! Well, if it is convenient, perhaps now is as good a time as ever. Doctor Howell, why don't you take a look at the supplies in the lab? The nurse can assist you if you need something. And while you're doing that, I'll walk our visiting firemen to the door."

"Doctor Howell, she's, well, she has a unique personality, it seems," Doctor Landis said cautiously once they were outside his office building. "I was a greenhorn back when I listened to her lecture. I didn't realize...."

"Yes, yes she is. She'll come across as distant, even arrogant at times, but she's focused like no one I've ever met," Horace said. "Isn't that right, Theo?"

"That about sums her up," Theo said, not wanting to commit himself. "And I'm sure my brother will say she's perfectly sane." He was about to say something about a second opinion being warranted, but then thought better of it.

"That's helpful. Doctors, thank you both. It's quite a day in Saugatuck's medical history to have two famous surgeons and a noted forensic pathologist here together. In my hospital, no less! Must be like when Bix Beiderbeck got together with King Oliver and Ruth Etting for a session. You should have been there. Now that was a memorable night," Doctor Landis said, shaking hands with Theo and then Horace.

"Well, looks like we might as well go back to your boat and await Beatrix's verdict," Horace said. "By the way, Theo, who was he talking about? That King fellow and the others? I've never heard of them."

"That, Horace, does not surprise me. They're musicians."

"Oh."

THE MURDER OF THE SAUGATUCK YARN HOARDER

CHAPTER FOUR

By the time Theo and Horace returned to the Aurora everyone except Mrs. Garwood was gone. "Let's see, Gar and Fred rented a little boat to go fishing," she told them. "More'n likely, they'll just drown worms and come home wanting something to eat. Harriet and Phoebe went up to Holland to do some shopping for a summer outfit. That girl's growing like a weed. So, it's just the two of you and me for right now."

"And, I've got my shopping to do because I'm not counting on Gar and Fred catching anything we can cook for dinner, so don't even think about mentioning your precious whitefish. You're on your own and you might be better off going out for lunch because I don't need you scrounging for food in my galley."

"That still leaves Clarice, remember?" Theo asked.

"Ah, yes, Mrs. Balfour, I almost forgot," Mrs. Garwood sighed. "She went out for a walk and said she would be back in a few minutes. That was about an hour and a half ago."

"Let me take one guess – she found a store that sells notions?" Theo asked.

"Notions, yarn and fabric," Mrs. Garwood said quietly.

"I thought as much. And just where do I find this store?" he asked.

"I think she said it was on one of the side streets between Butler and Water," she smiled. "I really didn't ask."

"Thank you, Mrs. G. I think I'll go check on her. Horace, you want to come along?" Theo asked.

"I appreciate the offer, but I think I'll enjoy a nice quiet time in my library. You go ahead. Standing around in a notions store is too much like sitting in a waiting room, only without chairs."

"You don't know what you're missing," Theo suggested.

"Oh, I think I do, and that's why the answer is still 'no.'"

"But think of it this way. It's good practice for the future. You know, in case your lady friend ever wants you to go shopping with her. Teaches you patience when you get stuck in your waiting room," Theo teased.

"That will do!" said Horace with a loud "Thunderation!" added for good measure. He stomped off to his library. What angered him more than the teasing was knowing that his brother was probably right. He enjoyed Beatrix' company, but if it evolved into something more, he would lose some of his independence. Shopping with her was not something he had considered before. He reached for his collection of Sherlock Holmes stories, turning to "The Adventure of the Speckled Band."

Theo found Clarice still in the shop looking at yarn. "You know, you've already got enough yarn to last a couple of life-times," he reminded her gently.

"Yes, I know," she answered absently, running her fingers over a skein. "They're all so lovely, don't you think? So soft. Wouldn't this make a lovely sweater? It's an adorable color." She turned to him and asked. "Would you wear a sweater of this yarn if I knitted it for you?"

"Yes, but isn't it a lot like all the yarn you already have at home? And, in our cabin. What are you going to do with all the stuff you already have? You don't even knit very much anymore."

"Yes, dear, I know. But it has such a soft gentle feel. Besides, a lady never reveals how much yarn she really owns." She took his hand to guide his fingers over the skein of grey yarn, then picked it up to inhale the aroma. "I'll just be a few more minutes. Why don't you and Horace find a bench, and I'll be right out."

"Horace is on the boat," Theo told her, realizing it was a futile battle of wills. The shop full of yarn had put her almost into a far-away trance. She wasn't even listening to him.

"Oh, that's nice. Well, why don't you enjoy the fresh air? I'll be just a few more minutes," she said in a trance-like voice.

Echoing his brother's expletive, Theo muttered "Thunderation!" and quickly left the shop. The promised "in a few minutes'"could be an hour or more. The sidewalk bench was across the street, and he took up residence, keeping a sharp eye on the door. Less than ten minutes later, Clarice slowly walked out the door and crossed the street.

"You didn't buy anything," Theo observed, somewhat relieved.

"No. No, as you said, I have enough yarn as it is," she said brightly.

"So, why did you go there?"

"For one thing, I enjoy looking even if I don't intend to buy some-thing. Men buy; women shop. And, for another, when you and Hor-ace and Beatrix mentioned all of the yarn that Miss Nason had in her house, well, what better place to learn about her than at a store that sells yarn?

"You're going to become a private eye if you're not careful," he teased.

"No dear, I leave that to you and your brother, and Beatrix," she said.

"So, what did you find out?" Theo asked.

"For starters, the owner said she just lost her best customer."

"That's it? Nothing more?"

"That's it. No one else said anything about Miss Nason."

"In other words, you didn't find out anything?"

"Theodore Balfour! Just the opposite. There were five women in that shop, all sharing a common interest in knitting and yarn, four of them very familiar with Miss Nason, and just the day after she died, remember. Every single one of them knows plenty and not one of them wanted to talk about it, about her, at least not while I was in the shop. I think that is strange, don't you?"

"So, why didn't you ask a few questions and find out something?"

"I might have scared them off. I'm biding my time. They saw me, spoke to me, and know I'm interested in yarn. Now we wait. I think Beatrix is right. There are too many secrets."

Theo considered what his wife had just told him, and realized she was probably right, even if he didn't quite see the logic in it at first. Finally he asked, "A conspiracy of silence? Guilt, even? That is suspicious!"

"Not necessarily. They've closed ranks, and they don't want to discuss it with a stranger, especially not a stranger whose husband, brother-in-law, and lady friend seem to become private eyes every time they come to town. What I think they're worried about is that it wasn't an accidental death. They have an idea it was not a natural death, and they're not going to talk with me about it – yet. Don't go jumping to conclusions."

"I don't see why they had to circle the wagons and close ranks," Theo objected. "It's not like someone is out to bump off a bunch of yarn-hoarders." Clarice didn't answer. He stood up and stretched slightly. "Well, lunch, my dear? Mrs. Garwood said we are on our own."

Beatrix returned mid-afternoon, broadly smiling, as she came into Horace's library and sat down. "You've had an interesting day,

I take it?" he asked, delighted to experience one of her few openly joyful moments.

"Yes, very interesting. I very much enjoyed working with Doctor Landis, and we came to some conclusions. It was just like when I was working in the laboratory in the Cities," she said. "A day in the lab is thirsty work, and I am very sure you know precisely what I have in mind." She waited for him to pour her a drink.

"Well?"

"For starters, just as I expected, none of the tissue or the swabs showed any indication of smoke inhalation. Nor was there any indication in the nodes we took from the lungs. She had received the blow on the head and was unconscious on the floor before the smoke got as far as her storage room."

"Good work. And?" Horace asked.

"We know she didn't die of smoke inhalation, but we still have no way of knowing whether she accidently pulled the shelf down on top of herself, or whether someone else pushed it, or if she was struck by the proverbial blunt object."

"So, still no way to tell whether it was murder or not? Thunderation!"

"Not yet, but I suspect that will soon change," she smiled.

"How?"

"Doctor Landis agreed that the cause of death has to be listed as 'suspicious'. He filled out the death certificate and signed it."

"Garrison will have a fit!" Horace moaned. "As Fred would say, you're dropping a hand grenade down his stove pipe."

"Past tense! Garrison had a fit. I went with Doctor Landis over to the police station. Garrison yelled and screamed at him, stamping his feet as if he were a child having a temper tantrum. Of course, he blamed it all on me. His bad behavior reminded me why I am very thankful I never yielded to any errant maternal instincts or became a GP. There is nothing he can do to change it, the certificate, that is, so he will have to investigate much more thoroughly. I do not believe it is something he enjoys. The man is obviously too hot-headed and aggressive for a careful investigation of any crime.

"So, I believe it is favorable news. And Horace, if you are offering a refill I will not refuse."

He got up to open his cabinet. "One or two fingers?" He asked, his back to her.

"Two, with water this time, please."

As he handed her the glass, Horace said, "You know what's going to happen, don't you? Garrison will yell, scream, and kick things around like a three-year-old child, and once he calms down he will be storming aboard my boat like the Barbary Pirates."

"Yes," she said demurely. "I believe he will. I think we can expect him at any time. Which puts the question back to you: What do you want to do, Horace? He cannot force us to investigate, you know. We could always just step back and refuse to do anything more." She looked at him, waiting for an answer. When he didn't respond, she said quietly, "Then, I suggest, that if the opportunity is offered, we say we will take the case. Horace, you know you enjoy it! You cannot resist the challenge and excitement. I think you even thrive on the challenge."

"You're probably right, Beatrix," he said thoughtfully. He took a sip and looked at her. "But I don't know..."

"Look, Horace, you and I saw something yesterday morning we have both seen a thousand times in our careers, and I never gave it a second thought. A woman, full of energy, full of life, and an hour later, dead. You and a million others saw too much of the same thing in France. I saw it again this morning with the autopsy. She may not have felt well, but she did not know she had a cancer that would probably kill her within the year. One way or another, that is our future, Horace – dead. I do not want to die in a hospital bed full of regrets. Do you?"

"No. But look, Beatrix, we both had very successful careers. We're a couple of old-timers, and all those youngsters we helped train are trying to push us off into the wings. You got pushed into retirement a few years back, and I've got these youngsters trying to do it to me now. I'm not doing nearly the amount of surgery I did a few years ago, and it certainly isn't challenging work when I do operate. I get bread and butter work, and then first assistants watching to make sure I don't make a mistake. Last fall I was so bored, I came down here when Phoebe wrote about three dead crows. So did you. I could have written an answer to her to explain what happened. You could have done the same thing. We didn't, or at least I didn't. I was just plain at loose ends."

"That is my point. We jumped at the chance for a bit of an adventure, and any moment now we are going to be offered another one. We can take it, or we can sit on a park bench, or perhaps you can see yourself spending your last days on a beach in Florida?" she asked. "Is that your idea of winding up your last years?"

"We could always go off to darkest Africa and work with Schweitzer. Now, that would be an adventure!"

"Horace, be serious. A year ago a client came in with a painting she had bought in London, and wanted me to do some investigative work. While she was there, she said she had picked up a magazine that had a mystery story in it with a woman amateur detective. An older woman. It was written by the same author you were reading last fall – Agatha Christie. The detective's name was Jane Marple."

"I take it you are going somewhere with this?" Horace asked, perplexed by the turn in their conversation.

"I am! I read the story, and I liked it very much. We have a choice on how we are going to invest whatever time we have left in life, and years have nothing to do with it."

"All right. If Garrison asks, we'll look into it," he said, raising his hands.

"Good." She held up her glass in a toast to their decision. "To Holmes and Adler."

Outside and down on the street, a car door slammed. "Holmes, I believe the game's afoot!" she smiled. She quickly finished her glass and handed it back to Horace. "Ditch the evidence before the coppers get here," she giggled.

"And Beatrix, how many times do I have to tell you that Holmes said that to Watson? 'Watson, the game's afoot.' He never said it to Irene Adler."

Garrison wasted no time asking to come aboard the Aurora. He stormed up the gangplank and summoned Horace and Beatrix onto the deck with a shout of "Front and center!" When they stood in front of him he snarled, "I don't know why you did it or how you did it, but somehow you convinced Landis to list the deceased's death as suspicious! It was a nice simple matter of a kitchen fire and, on the other side of the house, the victim. Open and shut. She smelled the fire, she tried to hide. Something happened and she got crushed by that wood rack! Nice, neat, simple! I swear, you put him up to it! Well, now I'm going to have to do an investigation and waste a lot of time and a lot of the taxpayers' money, and I'm not happy about it."

"No, I can see that," Horace said calmly, trying not to smile. "You do seem a little out of sorts this afternoon."

"So, I want you to talk some common sense into Doc Landis and have him change his report!"

"No, "Beatrix said firmly.

"No." Horace echoed her answer.

The chief stepped up to her, inches from her face. "Really? Smells to me like you've had some alcohol. Maybe that's what's clouding your thinking. I could run you in for possessing booze."

"Oh, I doubt it. I prescribed it for Doctor Howell, Chief. All perfectly legal according to the Volstead Act," Horace told him.

"As I did for Doctor Horace Balfour," replied Beatrix. "It's almost too bad you're not a preacher. We could prescribe some for you, too."

The chief's face reddened in fury. "Fine! Be that as it may. Well, I'm making you my investigators on this case. You started it, you finish it! Is that clear?"

"Perfectly, Chief," Beatrix said. "We will need full access to the house. I want you to go up and cordon it off. No one goes in but us."

The chief turned his back to leave, shouting, "Fine! If that's what it takes! Have it your way! I'll have the property posted!" He stormed down the gangplank.

"Say, Chief. What about expenses?" Horace taunted him.

"And a retainer and per diem," Beatrix teased.

"Go to blazes! Just get this thing wrapped up before everyone thinks there is a murderer on the loose! It's bad for the tourist business. The mayor doesn't like it. Solve it! You hear?"

The tires on his car squealed as he pulled away.

"I'd say we have our adventure, Irene," Horace said quietly. "I can't wait to tell Fred and Theo. What does he mean a murderer on the loose, anyway?"

Beatrix reverted to her absent, far-away persona. "It is a small town. There is always talk when there has been an unexpected and unexplained death. And, if there is not an actual murder, people must be convinced it was not merely brushed under the rug." She walked stiffly across the deck and down the stairs to her cabin. She turned to tell Horace, "You heard the chief. It's bad for business, so it is too easy to try to sweep it away."

An hour or so before the time Mrs. Garwood planned to serve dinner, Theo and Clarice, Fred, Harriet, and Beatrix joined Horace in his library. "Well, I suspect we all have tales of great adventure and hi-jinks. Fred, let's start with you. I understand you went fishing."

He mumbled something about him and the captain getting three bottom-feeding carp and two suckers between them, "And we gave them away on account of the fact that the captain here done did say that his missus wouldn't touch them."

"For which we ought to be grateful," the captain added. "Bottom feeders taste like mud."

Horace moved on to Harriet, who talked about wandering in and out of the shops in Holland and finding a couple of summer dresses for Phoebe. Her throat tightened a bit as she added that Phoebe didn't like any of them because they were too young-looking for her tastes. Clarice reached over to put a hand on her arm: "Dear, the battle is just beginning."

After Clarice had talked about her visit to the yarn shop, and Theo didn't have much to add to the conversation, Horace smiled broadly. "Well, I believe our mundane life is about to change."

"Oh, no!" Theo moaned. "Horace!" He glanced at his brother and then looked at Beatrix who had her eyes down, smiling in pleasure. "Don't tell me."

"The autopsy was very clearly and carefully done, and Miss Nason's death could only be listed as 'suspicious'. Doctor Landis signed the document. Not Beatrix, not I. Landis. Just Landis."

"Let me guess," Theo interrupted. "Landis gave the certificate to Garrison, and Garrison shot over here, hot under the collar and about ready to burst a vein. He got here and you two just couldn't resist having an adventure, could you?"

"That just about sums it up. I don't think we should interrupt him for a while," Horace said firmly. "Beatrix and I probably saved him from a stroke or fatal heart attack. We've been volunteered to figure it out. There you have it."

"Conscripted you mean!" Theo retorted.

Beatrix looked up and said flatly, "I have some responsibility for this. I talked Horace into taking the case. If you must have someone to blame, then look to me for it."

Theo's mouth opened to say something but he wasn't able to form the words. Finally, he gave up, shaking his head in disgust. Clarice and Harriet were also stunned to silence, leaving only Fred to support his boss and Beatrix. Phoebe was quiet and torn between being proud of her grandfather and fearful of him working too closely with Beatrix.

"Now, just relax, Theo. The death certificate says 'suspicious' and nothing more. All we're going to do is look a little further into it, and that's it. A day or so, at the most. Think of it as a way to clear the cobwebs out of our brains," Horace said firmly.

"You know better than that, "Theo replied. "When you get bored, this is what happens. You two have been here less than a week, and you're already restless and stirring up mischief. Why in the world you can't take up fishing or something normal like that is beyond me. Golf, maybe. Chase a little white ball around and burn off some of that energy! Let me tell you, you'll look into this alright, and before anyone knows it, you'll think there is a murderer on the loose. I've seen it three times before, and we always end up on the business end of a gun. Well, one of these days our luck is going to run out. You hear me? Run out!"

"I've been thinking about that, and I'm inclined to think it's better to stare down a gun than die of boredom, and you know it," Horace said quietly. "You heard Landis this morning. The old girl had lung cancer and would have died in bed. That's not how I want to slither across the finish line."

"Yeah, and I know who put that idea in your head, too!"

"So, how do you like me so far?" Horace asked before Beatrix could say anything.

The question caught Theo off-guard, confused him for a moment, and he shot back, "Not much!"

"Good. So I take it you'll sign on with us.

"Us? Who's us? Never mind, I can figure out the answer to my own question."

"Well, Beatrix and I, of course, so far. But from the look of him, Fred's up for a bit of a diversion," Horace smiled genially.

"Yesirreebob, you bet I am! You'd be in a sorry state if I weren't, and you know it!" Fred chortled.

"I give up," Theo said. "You've had too much giggle juice to make any sense, if you ask me." He paused, his eyes narrowing as he looked at Beatrix and Horace, and muttered, "Ah, then count me in, too. If I don't go along I might miss something."

CHAPTER FIVE

When Mrs. Garwood rang the dinner gong Harriet turned to the others. "Now, please, let's not talk about any of this over dinner or around Phoebe. I don't want her dragged into this murder business, and I don't want her having nightmares thinking about Fairy, I mean, Miss Nason. That goes for all of us. We all keep quiet about it. Is that clear? Everyone agree?"

They agreed, but as dinner dragged on, the adults were getting restless for Phoebe to leave the table. Twice, Clarice had given her permission to go into the lounge to read or do something else, perhaps play the piano. The girl wasn't interested, and wanted to stay with the others, as close to her grandfather as possible. Finally, Harriet said that it was time for her to go to bed. "You're old enough to walk home on your own. Straight home, though, is that clear?"

Phoebe yawned, reluctantly agreed, and dutifully went around the table to give each of the adults a good night hug and kiss, saving her grandfather for last. "Still my best girl?" he asked.

"Best and ONLY girl," she replied firmly, giving a sideways glance toward Beatrix to make certain she heard it. Harriet caught the meaning, looked upward and silently said, "Thank you, Lord, and keep it that way, please."

As soon as Harriet could see Phoebe was halfway down the block on Water Street, she gave the all-clear, and all of them moved their chairs in a bit closer around the table, and kept their voices lowso they couldn't be heard from the sidewalk.

"Bet you already got a plan of attack, haven't you, Boss? Just like Pershing and Haig and all those other generals you hob-nobbed with," Fred whispered. "That's what your fellow generals done did!"

Beatrix interrupted, her eyes flashing with irritation. "I believe the first task is to carefully examine the Nason house."

"Especially the kitchen?" Horace asked.

"Definitely, the kitchen. We know the cause of death. It was a blow on the head. Right now, that is about all we know. We did not have the opportunity to look at the kitchen, much less the stove. The fire was obviously in that room, but we do not yet know the cause of it. The assumption is that she left the gas on and something caught on fire. We cannot jump to conclusions."

"That includes not jumping to the conclusion it was a murder," Harriet added.

"Fingerprints?" Theo asked.

"I doubt it would do us much good. The firemen were in and out of there, and the chief and who knows who else was there. Beatrix is right: We do the kitchen first," Horace said.

"And, what can I do to help?" Clarice asked. "Roll bandages?"

Horace's head shot up. "No, but close. Knit socks!"

"What! What do you mean? I did that during the war. Socks and scarves for the soldiers," she fired back at him. "Horace, you are no Will Rogers, so do not even try to be funny."

"You mentioned the yarn shop and the women around here who knit. They're a wealth of information. I'm sure they would welcome a newcomer," Horace told her.

"How about being a dear and making it two newcomers? Phoebe could go with you," Harriet suggested. "Besides, now that school is out, it will give her something to do."

"Good idea! No one will suspect you're a spy if you bring her along. She'll be a diversion," Horace added.

"Thank-you. That will keep her safely out of the way and off the streets. And, if it turns out it was a murder, she won't be on her own if there is a killer on the loose. Thank-you!" Harriet said.

"So, what am I really supposed to do?" Clarice asked, still thinking they were teasing.

"Knit and listen, knit and listen, and once in a while ask some questions," Theo told her.

"Oh, I see. You are serious. Well, yes, of course, if you think it will help," Clarice said.

"There is one other thing," Beatrix said quietly, her eyes fixed on the dunes on the other side of the river. "Harriet, tell us about Miss Nason."

Harriet looked at her for a moment, uncomfortable at being put on the spot. "Well, she moved here a number of years ago, before we came here, and seemed to live comfortably. I mean, she didn't have to work, but I understand she did some teaching during the war, and then during the Spanish Flu epidemic because there was a shortage of teachers. I understand that no one liked her. I heard, but I'm not certain, she was a school teacher before she came here from somewhere in Iowa. I don't know all that she did, but she was involved in almost everything in the community at one time or another."

"One time or another?" Clarice asked.

Harriet blew the air out of her cheeks. "Well, the truth of the matter is, she wasn't very well liked because she was a regular little Miss Know-It-All and could be very outspoken." She paused and added softly, "She had a way of rubbing people the wrong way." She paused and added, "Everyone, always, and always the wrong way."

"I am sure that is an understatement," Beatrix said.

Harriet grimaced. "It is. It's just that I am uncomfortable saying, well, unkind things about the dead. Truth be told, she was a busybody and she was one of those bossy, nosey women who believed she was always right!

"We all know that type," Clarice said. "Go on."

"Well, if someone so much as dared to disagree with her, she could be ruthless. She'd say the most awful things about them, usually behind their backs, so no one dared to stand up to her. If she had it against you, she was like a rat terrier and never let go. That's how she got the nickname 'Fairy Nightshade'. She was always flitting around on her bicycle spewing her poison in all directions."

Again, Harriet took a long pause. "Look, if it does turn out that someone killed her, God forbid, there's not a woman in town who didn't say at least once they wished she would just dry up and die. A few of them said they'd gladly ditch her up on the side of the head with a skillet. More than once I wanted to turn her nose to twelve."

"That's interesting, using a skillet like that," Theo said. Then, turning to Clarice, "And don't you get any ideas, young lady!"

"I am not familiar with that phrase," Beatrix said. "It is impossible to turn someone's nose one hundred eighty degrees."

"It means I wanted to slap her face, and more than once, for things she said," Harriet answered.

Beatrix brightened up, "Oh, I understand. Some of the nurses and laboratory assistants at the hospital refer to it as giving someone, usually another woman, I believe, a good bitch-slapping."

"Beatrix! Thunderation, woman. That, coming out of you?" Horace asked.

"Well, I am only repeating what I heard," she said quietly. "I did not mean to offend."

"Not at all, not at all," Theo laughed, realizing he was beginning to warm up to her, if only incrementally for a moment.

"Harriet, go on," Horace urged.

"She was a difficult woman. She'd turn up at everything going on in town – churches, the Woman's Club, the village hall, even Ox-Bow, everywhere. And that includes at Village Council meetings. She was always butting in, criticizing that things weren't being done the right way. Oh, and at churches. I think she was a member of every church in town at one time or another. Even if she wasn't a member, she didn't hesitate to tell someone how things could be done better. One time she was sitting in front of a visitor. Well, apparently his back was hurting and he leaned forward a bit. Fairy Nightshade turned around, snapped her fingers, and told him to sit up straight when he was in church! Does that give you an idea about her?"

"Tell Grandfather about funerals," Phoebe blurted out. The sound of her voice startled everyone.

"I thought you were told to go home, young lady," Harriet said firmly. "How long have you been standing there listening to us?"

"Not long. I was going home, but then I got scared that maybe someone would hurt you if you were walking alone. I came back here to walk you home, and that way we'll both be safe," the girl said.

Harriet was about to reprimand her daughter, but stopped when Clarice put a hand on her arm. "I perfectly understand, dear," Clarice told Phoebe. "I think that was very thoughtful and wise of you. Both of you will be much safer walking together. You're a very thoughtful girl to look out for your mother like this.

The other adults at the table realized that it was really Phoebe who was afraid of being on her own. "Seems to me that if you're old enough to be thinking about your mother first, you can stay here for a while," Theo added.

Harriet smiled, and then continued. "Well, funerals: She went to every funeral in town, even if she didn't know the deceased. "

"That's odd," Horace said.

"Not really. She said she was there to be sure it was done right...," Harriet began.

Phoebe interrupted her, "And, she'd straighten out the flower arrangements because she said they were badly arranged! If a candle wasn't straight, she'd go right up in the middle of the service to straighten it. She did that one time at All Saints. At least that's what I heard."

Harriet shot her daughter a withering look, then continued, "But I think what she really wanted was to help herself to the food at the reception. Can you believe it? She'd be the first in line and fill her plate. Even while she was going through the line, she was commenting on the food, how it looked, how it was arranged, everything, and of course nothing was ever good enough or done correctly. She criticized everything. But then, after everyone had gone through the line, if there was still food on the table, she'd go through a second time and wrap up some to take home."

"How many ham buns can one woman eat?" Clarice asked, giggling.

"She'd get some food to take home and then light out of there on her bicycle," Harriet said. "We all dreaded seeing her coming our way, and we all loved seeing her go."

"Decoration Day, I saw her talking to Chief Garrison and the commander," Horace added.

"Well, no doubt she was telling the chief how to use the clutch on the car, and the commander how to get you boys to march in step," Harriet laughed.

"I would suspect then, that she was not popular," Beatrix observed

"And then she came over to where I was standing. So, is that why you came up to me and interrupted? You were rescuing me, weren't you?" Horace asked Phoebe. The girl beamed and nodded.

The more she talked, the more Harriet was confident speaking her mind. "She was vile, nasty, mean-spirited. She had an acid tongue and thought she was better than anyone else – and let us all know it. There! I've said my piece!"

For a few minutes they sat in silence, thinking over her remarks.

"Well, from the sound of it, every woman in town had good reason to want her dead," Horace said. "Seems like you all have a motive."

"Did she have any friends?" Beatrix asked.

"No, not really. Like I said, we gave her a wide berth and tried not to get involved. Most of us, at least. The only woman who spent any time with her was Bertha, Bertha Lee. Truth be told, I think Miss Nason was horrible to her," Harriet answered quietly. "We all felt sorry for her."

"Why?" Clarice asked.

"Bertha is one of those women who, well, I hate to say it, but she's pathetically clingy. She tries to please everyone. She wants everyone to be happy. I think Miss Nason saw it in her as a weakness and took advantage," Harriet said carefully.

"What do you mean?"

"I can't describe it very well. Seeing the two of them together was like watching a cat toy with a mouse. In fact, Miss Lee's nickname is

'Mouse.' Miss Nason batted her around, one minute, then the next told her what a good friend she was," Harriet explained. "And, Miss Nason would laugh and make fun of Miss Lee, even calling her The Mouse, behind her back."

"That is horrible!" Beatrix said. Horace was alarmed by the look of pain and sorrow in her eyes. Obviously, the conversation had touched a raw nerve.

"She made fun of her; the way she dressed, the way she walked, everything," Harriet added. "And, she could imitate her voice almost perfectly, just to hurt her."

"Indeed," Horace answered. "So, what you're saying is that every woman in town despised Fairy Nightshade. What about the men?"

"Let's just say that no man, at least not that I know of, ever turned up on her doorstep with a bunch of posies and a box of chocolate," Harriet said firmly. "One casual encounter with her was enough for most of them."

"And men do talk and gossip. I am sure the word soon spread," Beatrix said in a sad tone.

"Well, we do have our work cut out for us. Everyone in town is a potential suspect, assuming it is murder and not a genuine accident," Theo said glumly.

"Tomorrow, we start at Miss Nason's house," Beatrix said as she stood up. "I am retiring for the night. Good evening, all." She walked down the steps to her cabin. Horace was very certain something was troubling her.

THE MURDER OF THE SAUGATUCK YARN HOARDER

CHAPTER SIX

"Horace," Beatrix said when he joined her on the deck for breakfast a little after sunrise. She lifted a coffee cup to greet him. "Horace, I have been thinking about something you said last evening. You said that everyone is a potential suspect. There is good reason to believe you are right. There is also good reason to believe you are not the only person to think that way. We must resolve this very quickly or there is a chance neighbors will turn on each other. Fear can spread like contagion."

"You might be right," he said quietly, thinking it over.

"I am right, Horace," she said flatly. "And, everyone in town is a suspect. It would have been very easy for someone to appear at the Decoration Day events, then slip away from the crowd and lay in wait for her."

"And you have an idea, I hope?" he asked.

"Yes. I propose that you and I leave immediately to look at Miss Nason's house."

"Now? What about the others? They're not even up yet."

"Good. All the better. I prefer that we go now and get started before there are too many distractions," she said carefully.

He nodded in agreement. "I see what you mean. All right. We'll leave a note in the galley for them to join us there after they have had breakfast. Yes, sometimes Fred's enthusiasm gets a bit much."

"I was thinking about how sometimes your enthusiasm can be just as distracting. The two of us working together will potentially be more productive."

They had walked about a block when Horace cautiously said, "It seemed like something was troubling you last evening when we were on the deck." When she finally answered, it was a quiet "yes." He didn't pursue the topic, but had an idea that it had something to do with the past, and that it brought back unpleasant memories. She was not going to let him enter any further into her life, either past or present.

It was a cool early morning and for the most part the streets were deserted. "Horace, there is something very odd about this town," she said, abruptly changing the conversation.

"There are a lot of things odd about this town," he laughed.

"There are no alleys for the draymen to deliver goods."

"I see," he said, waiting for a further explanation. Finally, he asked, "Is there a connection?"

"Connection? Connection to what? The murder? To something else? No. Not at all. Just an observation, and I find it both odd and interesting no one thought of it when they laid out the streets," she said. They continued walking in silence, enjoying the quietness of a late May morning.

"So, what are we looking for?" Horace asked when they arrived at the house. "Obviously, evidence, but what evidence, but what else?"

"I don't know. We need to observe everything," she said as they stood on the sidewalk in front of the house.

"Well, I don't think we'll find anything out here," he said quietly.

"I agree, although there is hardly a need to whisper, Horace. We are not cat burglars and no one is around," she told him as they walked up to the front door.

"Well, what a surprise. The chief didn't even lock it," Horace said sarcastically. "Lead on, Beatrix."

The front parlor was immaculate and tastefully decorated. Despite the firemen and others who had rushed into the house to extinguish the fire, everything seemed perfect. "Someone has been in here and cleaned," Beatrix said. The chairs were set at an angle for conversation. Several magazines on the coffee table were neatly stacked. She pointed down to the hardwood floors, "Even the floor has been cleaned since the firemen and Chief Garrison were here. When we were here yesterday, there was trash in this basket," he added.

"I agree. It is too clean. The place looks like one of those model houses for sale," Horace barely whispered, almost as if a louder voice would somehow disturb the room. Beatrix visibly relaxed in the orderliness and perfection of the room.

Without thinking, when he noticed that the handle of one umbrella in the stand was in the opposite direction from the others, he turned it around to match the others. "Horace! Use your handkerchief and put it back exactly the way you found it. I want to examine it later." He restored it to its original position.

"The place is as neat as a pin," he repeated.

"An apt idiom for the homes of someone interested in textiles, even if it is another of your atrocious puns. William Thackery first used the phrase, 'Neat as a pin' in one of his novels in the last century. Machine-made pins were perfectly smooth and would not tear the fabric," she added, looking carefully at everything in the room, focusing on each piece, looking for something. She moved over to the bookcase near the fireplace. "Every book in uniform order," she said quietly. "Magnificent, isn't it?"

"No, I don't agree. Everything is in too perfect an order for the morning after a fire and suspicious death. There would have been firemen bursting in here, Garrison running around like a chicken with its head cut off, the undertakers, and no telling who else. Then look at this house. It's picture perfect. And the floor has been too well cleaned. Your love for order is blinding you, Beatrix,"

She stared at him for an uncomfortably long time, thinking through everything he had just said. "Yes, you may be right. And we must somehow determine if it was done out of respect for the deceased or to cover up or hide evidence. You make a very good point."

She silently moved on to the kitchen, standing motionless in the doorway, studying everything. With the exception of a cast iron skillet still on the stove, everything was in perfect order. Horace opened a silverware drawer, and commented that the knives were all facing the same direction, and the rest of the cutlery also in uniform order. Tea cloths had been perfectly folded and arranged; pots and pans carefully set in place.

"I rather like this woman," Beatrix said. "If only from the appearance of her house, I believe I might have enjoyed her company. There is a perfect pattern to everything. It is neat, tidy, and logical. A model of efficiency. Now, do not touch that skillet. That is the only thing that breaks the uniformity."

"Wouldn't think of it," Horace fibbed as he dropped his hand to his side.

"No, you would only do it without thinking. It is a very natural temptation because it is out of place, and it may be the solution to this murder. When Fred gets here, I want him to carefully take it out to the car so we can take it back to the boat to examine it later. Now, I want to look at her yarn room before the others get here." They moved down the hall and stood at the doorway. Beatrix lifted up her camera and took some pictures of the room. "Interesting," she said quietly.

The room had obviously once been immaculately maintained, much like the rest of the house. Three walls were lined with shelves, all of them containing yarn. The exception to the perfect orderliness was the top shelving unit that had somehow been pulled or pushed over, spilling skeins across the floor. Horace was still surprised at the huge collection of yarn, enough to last several lifetimes. It didn't make sense to him. How could anyone possibly use all of it, even if they knitted constantly? Why would anyone want such a vast collection?

Beatrix finished taking pictures and wanted to look at the rest of the house before the others joined them. The dining room was next, and from the brief time Beatrix spent there it didn't appear to offer anything out of the ordinary. Nor the half bath on the main floor.

There were two bedrooms upstairs, as well as a full bath, and they were as orderly and perfect as the rest of the house. Beatrix tried the knob on the bathroom closet door. "Locked. How very odd. I cannot understand why someone would choose to lock a closet door. The room door, perhaps, but a closet door is odd. This might prove interesting. Possibly she was not only orderly, but secretive, as well."

"A job for Fred when he gets here," Horace said

Beatrix said nothing while they were looking at the rooms, nor when they went back down the stairs. At the bottom, she abruptly sat on a step, staring straight ahead, silent. After Horace quietly said he thought he would go outside to look at the rest of the house, she murmured, "Enjoy your pipe, as well. I will call when I need you." He realized he had been dismissed.

Horace wandered slowly around the house, looking for anything that might indicate a break-in, or even someone snooping. "Casing the joint," he said out loud to himself. There was nothing. Like the inside, the clapboard-covered exterior was in perfect condition. It was almost too perfect, he thought to himself. No peeled paint anywhere; the window panes were puttied and the glass clean. It would have taken a full-time caretaker to keep even a house this small in such perfect order. And how, he wondered, would that have given Fairy Nightshade enough time to organize everyone's life. "Something is missing here," he muttered.

"Well, you thinking about buying the place?" Theo asked his brother when he and his wife and Fred arrived.

"Wouldn't be all that bad," Horace said, knocking the ashes out of his pipe. "Pretty enough, but you know, I'm certain there's something wrong. It's just too perfect."

"Is that what makes you think this was foul play?" Theo asked.

"Right now, I couldn't tell you one way or another."

Horace turned to Fred, asking him to pick the lock on the bathroom closet door, and then added that Beatrix had another project for him. The two brothers watched as Fred went inside. Clarice was hard on his heels.

"The odd thing is, it's as clean and organized as an operating theatre," Horace said to Theo. "It's the way an operating room should be, but this is almost like a museum or one of those houses in the slick magazines. It's too perfect."

"A bit too organized, even for Beatrix?" Theo asked.

"No, not for her," Horace said, smiling as he emptied out his pipe. The two men sat on the front steps of the house, waiting for Beatrix to summon them.

It was Clarice who called them when she came hurrying down the front steps and out to the porch. "Come quickly. Beatrix has found something."

Horace and Theo followed her up the stairs. "Picked it with ease," Fred said in triumph. He stepped aside as Beatrix opened the bathroom closet door. Inside were bankers' boxes stacked from floor to ceiling, each numbered by year.

"I believe we found a true treasure trove of information," Beatrix told them in almost reverential tones. "I looked in one, and if the others are like it, they contain diaries, financial accounts, and other information."

"No wonder she kept this room locked," Horace observed.

"They're all dated," said a stunned Theo, staring at the boxes. "Every single year."

"Yes, that was quite helpful of Miss Nason. Gentlemen, we need to take these back to the boat. If you please...."

"All of them?" Horace asked.

"All of them," she said firmly.

"And you are sure you need them?" Theo asked, instantly looking at the work ahead of them.

"You want us to carry them out to the car, then up the gangplank? And you're going to go through them all, is that it?"

"All of them. It's rather exciting, is it not? Do not be concerned about putting them in chronological order until we get to..." Beatrix froze, gasped, and put her hand over her mouth in dismay. "Horace, I must apologize. I forgot to ask permission first. I am very sorry. Will it be alright if we examine the contents in your library?"

"Of course! Hand me the first box, would you, Fred?"

Twenty-three trips up and down the stairs, one box at a time, and the task was finished. "I done did save enough room for the two of you to ride back, Doctor Theo, if you don't mind getting a little cozy."

"I certainly don't mind," Clarice teased Theo.

"And please be careful with the cane and frying pan, Fred. They may be evidence," Beatrix cautioned as they prepared to drive back.

"Now, if we take our time examining the rest of the house, all of those boxes should be in the library by the time we get back to the Aurora," Horace said with a smile

"I do so appreciate the way you think," Beatrix replied. "Now, please stay outside while I walk through the house one more time."

CHAPTER SEVEN

"Where shall we start?" Horace asked Beatrix, once they got back to the boat late that morning. "Cane, skillet, or boxes?

"I will start with that cane you thought was an umbrella," she said flatly. "Alone. I may need your assistance when we get to the skillet. Please do not wander too far off." She nodded toward the door of his library, indicating it was time for him to leave her to get on with her work.

Horace went out on the deck and sat down next to his brother. "Most naughty boys get sent to their room; you seem to get kicked out," Theo teased. "Have you noticed she does that pretty often to you?"

"That'll do," Horace said firmly. "She's like me. We both like our solitude at times."

"So, tell me what you think? Accident or murder?"

"Depends on what she finds on that cane and then we get to the skillet. Maybe, maybe not. If she finds something, and if it's important, then we'll know. That's my guess at the moment. Right now I'm not certain one way or the other."

"Why the cane?" Theo asked.

"It was in an umbrella stand near the front door. It was the only cane in there, and the only handle turned the wrong way from the others. The rest were umbrellas."

"And that somehow makes it a clue?" Theo asked, his right eyebrow raised, and he squinted with his left in disbelief.

"Not necessarily, at least not to you or me. Beatrix sees patterns, and this didn't fit the pattern. To her, it was worth investigating," Horace explained.

"My money is still on an accident. I have a hunch she put something on the stove and then went into that yarn room to look at something high up on a shelf and pulled it down on top of herself. And, since you said it was the only cane in a stand full of umbrellas, maybe that's how she separated them. It's the simplest and most logical explanation," Theo said, staring absently across the river. "After that, someone noticed the smoke and fire, and everyone was spared listening to your speech."

"You might be right. It is logical and it makes sense. Just remember, Beatrix is a forensic pathologist, and she has a different perspective that sometimes seems strange," Horace said. "She can find connections the rest of us miss."

"Well, the strange part is right, at least."

Horace ignored the comment and pulled out his pipe. For half an hour the brothers sat wordlessly staring at the water, lost in their own thoughts until Beatrix joined them.

"Well?" Horace asked.

"Nothing. I had hoped I might see some recent damage or scratches on the handle or the bottom, a dent, anything but there was nothing. I looked, of course, at it from different angles and in different light, but there is nothing. Our hopes are dashed for the cane giving us a clue," she told them. She held out her hand, wanting Horace's pipe.

"Why were you expecting to find something?" Theo asked.

She exhaled a large plume of smoke. "Simply because it was the only object that broke the pattern in the front parlor. Everything else was uniform. In some ways, the furnishings are almost balanced or symmetrical. Perhaps it was used to bash Miss Nason over the head, but there is no evidence. I believe it is what Fred would call a 'long shot.' Horace, if you are ready, we can move on to the skillet. I will need your assistance. Theo, you are welcome to observe." For a second Beatrix held out her hand to help Horace out of the chair, then quickly withdrew it and hurried ahead of him back to the library. Theo declined the invitation.

"I have never seen a skillet in this condition. It is almost as if someone burned it partially through the middle. Look at it. It is burnt from the top, not the bottom," Beatrix said, pointing at the pan. "It is almost impossible to burn a cast iron frying pan." She handed Horace the magnifying glass.

He studied the pan for a few minutes, turning it in different directions under the light. "That is odd. And then there are these little flecks of red just below the rim. It looks like a few fibers of cloth. Yarn, might be the answer, considering what we saw in the store room." He moved out of the way so Beatrix could examine it.

She looked up. "This could have been done by a welding torch, but that would not account for the red flakes and these fibres. Besides, why would someone take a welding torch to the inside of a frying pan? That is not rational, and the burn pattern is not consistent with a torch. What would do it?" She didn't wait for an answer, and began very carefully scraping the blade of a pocket knife against the inside of the skillet. When she had collected some of the residue, she carefully put it on a piece of white paper.

"She was meticulous," Horace observed. "I don't see any food."

"Nor is there any residue of cooking grease. That means that there was nothing cooking on the stove when she was at the parade, nor when she returned," Beatrix answered. "So, it was not a traditional kitchen fire. Another possibility is that it was scrubbed and cleaned by whomever tidied the rest of the house."

"And that makes it all the more confusing. The chief and the firemen all said the skillet was on the burner and the gas was turned on. Something had to have been in the pan because we smelled the smoke, but even if it was red hot, it wouldn't have burned from the inside like this. The only logical conclusion is that something was in here that burned. It was either when she returned, or else...."

"Or else someone burned something in it. But what would burn that hot? What would give off that stench?"

"Well, we both know that magnesium burns white hot. Mix it with aluminium powder, and...." Horace began slowly.

"And that would have left a white residue. Not red. Nor can we forget these tiny pieces of fibre," Beatrix interrupted.

"What about phosphorous?" Horace asked.

"White again, remember?" She finished scraping the inside of the pan, shook a little more residue into the center of the paper, and carefully emptied it into a glass Petri dish with a cover. She turned and looked blankly at him. "I need to think," she said quietly.

Horace took it as an invitation to leave.

Theo and Phoebe were in their deck chairs when Horace ambled across the deck. "Pull up a chair. I was trying to talk your granddaughter into going fishing, but she says she has some plans."

"I don't like worms," Phoebe said. "They're icky!"

"That's funny. Most fish love a nice worm dinner. They're practically hooked on them," Theo teased, laughing at his own pun. Phoebe understood his little joke and gave him a squint-eyed withering glare.

"I'll go fishing but only if I don't have to put a worm on the hook. Or take a fish off the hook. Or clean it," she said firmly, almost defiantly, counting each response on a finger.

"But you might consent to eat fish?" Theo asked.

"Well... maybe," she said quietly. "I'll eat it if Mrs. Garwood cooks it!"

"I see," Horace said. "So, what do you want to do?"

"I thought I could help you solve the Fairy Nightshade murder case!"

"Now, just what makes you think it is a murder, Phoebe?"

"Because that's what everyone is saying. They say she was murdered in broad daylight right in her own home. And then when they heard that you were working on the case, they just knew it had to be a murder. You are going to solve it, aren't you, Grandfather? I told my friend Janie Bird that you could solve it. And my friends Stu and Henry think you're aces when it comes to solving murders, so you have to do it!"

"First we have to be sure it was murder and not an accident. That's what Doctor Howell is working on right now. If it was an accident, well then, that's the end of it. And if it wasn't an accident, then I guess we'll have to figure out who did it."

"But it has to be a murder! It just has to be! That's what everyone is saying, and they are scared the murderer might be hiding in plain sight!" she practically wailed. "Maybe it is someone I know, or Mother knows! That's why I want to help. Can I, please? Please, can I?"

He didn't answer at first, and avoided the fierce glare from his brother who was obviously opposed to that idea. To stall for time, he pulled out tobacco pouch and pipe, and carefully filled it. "There is something you can do, if it is a possible murder. And remember, we don't know that for sure, understood?"

"Yes," she said eagerly, shifting a bit closer to him and leaning closer.

"If, and that is still a big 'if', remember, I need a spy."

"A spy? With a badge and gun and everything?" she asked.

"No, that is a policeman or a private eye detective. A spy goes undercover, and a really good spy is someone who never lets on that they are a spy. What spies mainly do is listen. They keep their eyes and ears open, always listening and watching for a clue."

Horace saw Theo shake his head and roll his eyes in disdain. "Think you could do that if we need you?"

"You bet I can!"

"Good. Great! So, what can you tell me about our Fairy Nightshade?" Horace asked. "What do you already know?"

Phoebe paused for a few moments. "Well, none of my friends really liked her. I mean, everyone was polite to her because we're supposed to be polite, aren't we? You know, especially if it is an adult. But no one ever liked her. Mother and I would cross the street if we saw her coming, and then look in a store window. You know, things like that."

"That part I think I already understand. But think back to last fall when you observed those crows. You were very specific about what you saw. That's what we need now," he told her.

"Oh!" she said brightly, and for the next few minutes told her grandfather how Fairy Nightshade had upbraided some of her friends for bad posture, and how she had told another friend she needed to do something about her hair. "And," she concluded, "when she came to our church, she told the minister's son he ought to know better than to pray with his eyes open. They're supposed to be closed. Does that help?"

"Yes, Phoebe, it does. It gives me a very good idea what the woman was like." Horace said. He was frustrated she was merely repeating what he already knew. "We'll need more, you know."

"And now you understand why nobody in town was her friend. Well, except for the Mouse."

"The Mouse? Does she have a name?" Even though Horace had heard the name before and knew some of the details of the story, he wanted Phoebe's perspective.

"It's Bertha Lee. Miss Lee. She always acts like a scared little house mouse, and she was always doing whatever Fairy Nightshade wanted her to do, so that's why she's called the Mouse.

With that, Phoebe jumped up from her chair and said she had to go to the library before it closed.

"Nice woman, this Nightshade dame," Theo observed. "Makes your girlfriend look like a genuine charmer."

"That will do," Horace growled at him.

"You ever wonder why this place has so many interesting characters? Think there is something in the water?" Theo asked.

"Thunderation, it's no different here than anywhere else. You think of some of the folks back home, including a few of our doctors and staff. Some of them have some real quirks, and you know it. But, we put up with them, same as folks do anywhere. Besides, in a big city they get lost in a crowd. A small town, and they stand out. Then you include the artists out to Ox-Bow and all the day-trippers, and it adds up."

"So far, I still think it is just an accidental death, and not much more," Theo yawned, then closed his eyes, not waiting for an answer.

CHAPTER EIGHT

Just after the first dinner gong Beatrix came out of Horace's library, slowly walked across the deck, and slumped into a chair next to him and Theo. "We have a few minutes before dinner, do we not?"

"Any luck?" Horace asked her quietly, concerned at her apparent exhaustion.

"No," she answered flatly. "I studied the scrapings. There are definitely some bits of fiber. Oh, I used your microscope. I hope you do not mind my using it without your prior permission. The fiber is not like anything normally found in most garments, although I think it may be either silk or satin."

"What about the little flecks of red?" Horace asked.

"A mystery. A complete mystery. I am quite certain they are non-organic, but beyond that...."

"Well, give it a rest, Beatrix. It's amazing what taking a break from it can do," Theo said gently.

"I believe you have been reading Sherlock Holmes, Theo. He would sometimes play his violin for hours, making the most awful sounds, while his mind was relaxing and finding the answer to a challenging case," Beatrix told him. "He found it helpful, although I believe it could be very irritating to Doctor Watson. Perhaps, Horace, we should take up the violin." A slight wink and a finger across the right side of her nose to Horace told him she was teasing and baiting his brother.

"You two do know that Sherlock Holmes is fictional, I hope?" Theo asked.

"Oh dear," Horace moaned. "Irene, if my brother is right, then that would make you a figment of my imagination. And here I thought you were real." He winked at her.

"Oh, but I am as very real as you, Sherlock. And, isn't your brother's real name, 'Mycroft'?" She gently bantered back. "Now, any idea what we might be having for dinner? I believe it is red meat of some type." She sniffed the air and jumped up. "I must see Mrs. Garwood before she washes the pan!"

Theo gave his brother a withering look that concluded with a raised eyebrow. "As I said, this town seems to attract an assortment of strange characters."

"Relax, little brother. I see the pattern," Horace told him. "She wants some of the scrapings from the pan to compare with the flakes from Fairy Nightshade's skillet."

"Well yes, of course. Perfectly reasonable," he said sarcastically.

Beatrix's plan to examine the inside bottom of one of Mrs. Garwood's best pans was not well received. "I'll not have you ruining it with your knives and chemicals and things," she snapped at her.

"I assure you it will not be ruined. I merely need a few burnt pieces."

"Burnt pieces! Woman and girl, I have never once in my life burnt a good piece of meat. You'll not find anything burnt on my pans!" Mrs. Garwood retorted.

"All the better, I can take some scrapings and burn them myself when you clean the pan," Beatrix said firmly, staring down Mrs Garwood until she relented. Beatrix returned to the deck chairs, telling Horace and Theo, "I will be working after dinner."

Once they had finished their meal, without waiting for dessert, much less excusing herself, Beatrix silently got up from the table, collected the pan from the galley, and motioned for Horace to join her. "Fortunately, there are sufficient pieces of this roast to test at different temperatures," she began. She held out her hand for a box of matches to light the Bunsen burner. When Horace asked what she was hoping to discover, Beatrix ignored him and focused on her work.

It was nearing sunset, hours later, when the two of them found Theo, Clarice and Fred sitting on the deck watching the sun migrate behind the dunes. She joined them. "I am convinced the red substance is inorganic."

"Which tells us what?" Theo asked.

"That it is inorganic, and it still remains a mystery."

"Well, you've put in a long day; time to quit. I know Fred won't turn down an offer to walk over to the drugstore for some ice cream before it closes. Want to join us?" Horace asked. Both Theo and Clarice declined.

"And your granddaughter Phoebe is not here with you? I am surprised," Beatrix said.

"Oh, she's probably off with friends. She's growing up," Horace said sadly.

"Ice cream it is, then. It is not often I get to step out with two gentlemen," she said with unusual brightness. "I hope by ice cream you did not mean one of your horrible Green River drinks. Horace, I think they are most unpleasant."

As they were turning the corner at the White House as Horace pulled out his pipe and matches. He was ready to light it when Beatrix commanded, "Stop! Let me see those matches!" The three of them stood in the middle of the sidewalk as Beatrix held up a single match and studied it carefully.

"It was murder! There is no doubt in my mind. It was murder! Miss Nason was killed by someone. It was no accident. Now we know for certain!" Beatrix's voice was vibrant with excitement, her eyes flashing.

"You figured that out by looking at a match?" Fred asked.

She ignored him. "We must go back to the boat. No, I misspoke. I must go back to the boat and work on this. Please, do not let me interrupt your plans!" she said. "Horace, do you have another box of matches with you?"

She watched as he patted his pockets, finally producing two small boxes. "Good!" She took one of them out of his hand and slipped it into her handbag. "I will need them. If you wish, I will replace them in the morning. Please, go enjoy your Green River."

Beatrix didn't wait for his answer. Once again, she was onto something, something important and completely oblivious to anything else. She turned on her heels and walked rapidly down the sidewalk toward the Aurora, leaving Fred and Horace behind on the corner, puzzled at her comments. "So, how'd she figure it was murder by looking at a match? That's what I'd like to know!" Fred said.

"I'd like to know that, too. Right now, I'm not certain. We'll find out when she's ready to tell us. You still want your ice cream or should we see what she's up to?"

"If you don't mind me saying so, Doc, I'd like to know how she solved a murder mystery by seeing you almost light your pipe. I can't always figure that there woman out."

"Fred, I can't figure out the way her mind works, and I probably know her better than most people. All I know is that she is brilliant and can see patterns and connections better and far faster than anyone I know, and that includes my brother. She can see things the rest of us miss."

"Yeah, I can see that in her, but she isn't much for having fun and sitting down to visit. I guess that's why you two get along so well. You're not much for fun, either. But I'll tell you something, and I hope you don't get up a head of steam on account of it, but she'd sure scare me off from asking her to step out with me."

Horace didn't answer until they were near the boat. "We're good friends, Fred. Beatrix and I have been that way for decades. And I think that is enough said."

Beatrix was already in Horace's library, scraping away at a couple of matches and collecting the bits into a Petri dish. "I trust you have a ceramic mortar and pedestal here," she said without looking up.

"Behind you on the shelf."

Beatrix took them and ground the scraping from the matches into a powder, then fixed a slide and put it into the holder on the microscope. She took out the slide, replacing it with one she had made from the scrapings in the cast iron skillet, then repeated her work a second time.

Finally, she looked up beaming. "It was murder. We solved it, Horace. The evidence is here! All we have to do is find who did it."

"What evidence?" Horace and Fred asked in unison.

"The fire. Fred, please find and bring Doctor Theo in here."

Horace nodded to Fred to bring in his brother.

When they returned, Beatrix began explaining that Fairy Nightshade had been murdered, and she had found the cause of the fire. "Phosphorous!" she said in triumph.

"Slow down, Beatrix. Phosphorous is white, and it ignites when it is exposed to air, but what you've got there is red. That doesn't add up," Theo said. "Besides, where would someone get phosphorous around here?"

Fred interrupted. "Say now, that's easy. Easy to make, but it's sorta kinda dangerous. It isn't that hard to do if you don't mind taking a chance on getting killed doing it!"

"Go on," Horace said. "Tell us how you know how to make phosphorus."

"Back during the war a squad of Tommies done got themselves captured by the Hun..."

"Some British soldiers were captured by the Germans," Horace translated for Beatrix.

"And they got thrown in the hoosegow, and didn't much like it."

"Jail, prisoner of war camp," Horace interrupted.

"Well, one of them officers had studied chemistry when he was at school, and was what you'd call a regular juvenile delinquent, and he said he knew how to catch the Huns with their pants down...."

"That part I understand," Beatrix said, smiling.

"And he knew how to make some homemade phosphorous," Fred continued.

"What?" the three of them asked together.

"He knew how to make some homemade phosphorous, which they done did, and when they had enough of it, and they was good and ready, one night they gave the Huns a nasty surprise. Well, it worked all right, because those boys nearly burned down the whole camp while they beat it out of there on the double-quick. I heard most of them made it back to their lines."

"Fred, is this some tall tale with a forever-lost formula?"

"No Sir, General. It's the honest truth. I heard it from the Tommy that done did it and saw the medal some French general gave him. Fact of the matter is, you took some shrapnel out of his legs a couple of months after he done did his get-away!" Fred said with a broad smile.

"And Fred, do you happen to know just how he made it?" Beatrix asked.

"Yes, Ma'am I sure do. Now, I have to tell you, I never got around to trying it once we got back to home on account of the fact I didn't want to burn down something, and I didn't rightly have any good reason to fool around with it. But I heard it works, and that's a fact!"

She pushed a pen and paper in his direction. "Please write it down for me."

Fred did, and pushed the paper back to her.

"Well, it's a bit unpleasant. But you are sure it works?" she asked.

"Sure as you're sitting there!" he replied. "Thing is, though, like I've been saying, this homemade stuff isn't exactly what you'd call any too stable, leastwise not for a while. And, it isn't nearly as powerful as the stuff the army uses, but it'll do the trick in a pinch. But, you leave it sitting in water too long and it turns red."

There was a long silence. "Red phosphorus is used in matches because it's stable. It burns hot but it needs something to ignite it. " Horace said slowly. "Like the sandpaper on a match box. Well I'll be. And you're sure that this formula works?"

"Sure does!" Fred said again.

"So, we assume somebody else knew how to make phosphorus, let it sit for a while until it turned red, then took it to Fairy Nightshade's house and put it on the stove and turned up the flame,"

Horace said slowly, trying to see his way through the steps. "It still seems like a bit of a stretch, to me."

"That means it was intentional, very deliberate, and at the very least, attempted arson," Beatrix added.

"Alright, hold on, both of you. Assuming that's right, that this formula works, and that's what happened, we've probably got arson, but that doesn't mean it was murder, and it doesn't get us one step closer to who did it!" Theo objected.

"No, Theo," Horace said, "If this is what was used to start the fire, then it was very intentional. It is definitely arson. Premeditated arson. The only question is whether it was unintentional homicide or premeditated murder. Right now, I think it's a mystery man behind all of this. He's at least a suspect in my book."

"Slow down, all of you," Theo snapped at them. "Assuming that's what the killer did, it seems it would have been a whole lot easier just to buy a couple of boxes of kitchen matches and scrape off the phosphorous without cooking the stuff up. That's doing it the hard way."

"Someone with intense hatred would have made a ritual of making their own phosphorous," Beatrix countered quietly. "Someone who wanted to inflict tremendous emotional pain. Someone with a sadistic bent."

For a few moments they stood silently, glaring at each other. "Well, I can tell you for sure, it isn't no woman that done did it," Fred retorted.

"Fred might be on to something. Poison is a woman's weapon of choice. Or, maybe a gun. But I can't see a woman committing murder like this," Theo agreed.

"And I think you are a blithering idiot to so quickly and cavalierly say such a thing!" Beatrix snapped. "A woman is as perfectly capable of simple chemistry as a man, and we can be far more devious and vicious when we are given just cause!" She paused and added, "Thus spake Irene!"

Horace stifled a chortle with a cough. "Theo I think you just got your tail feathers singed."

"Yeah, I'd say so, and well deserved. Beatrix, please accept my apologies," Theo said quietly.

"We need to see if this formula works, so tomorrow morning, gentlemen, I need some specimens from you; one from each of you. First thing," Beatrix said as she left the library. She paused at the door. "First thing, or else I will personally supervise the collection of samples." The three men did not see the smile on her face as she returned to her cabin.

CHAPTER NINE

"You got some idea where I ought to put Doctor Howell's, ah, her, ah, scientific medical experiment while it ages for a while?" Fred asked Doctor Horace, holding up a quart jar. "It's got to sit for at least a week."

"Somewhere out of the way where it won't get knocked over. And preferably well down wind," he replied. "If I were you, I wouldn't dare ask Mrs. Garwood if she has a spot for it in her galley, or we'll all regret it."

Fred nodded. "You're sure right about that! She'd have a fit if I so much as asked. Maybe down in the engine room. Ought to be out of the way there behind the boilers."

"Just don't forget where you put it. We don't want to discover it once it has over-ripened."

"Yes, sir!"

"And then scout around town to see if there is someplace safe we can try out your recipe. And, I don't mean on my boat!"

"That's right good thinking, Boss, seeing as how that stuff isn't any too stable once we finish it off."

"And don't forget to wash up after you store that," Horace reminded him.

"Yeah, pretty dirty down in that engine room," Fred smiled, teasing his employer.

"I didn't get a chance to apologize for what Theo said last evening," Horace told Beatrix. "Nor did I do anything to clamp down on him. I am very sorry."

She held up a hand. "There is no need. Statistically, his observation was completely accurate, although I found it very prejudicial. A woman is just as capable as any man when it comes to anything. I reacted without thinking. It is a new day; let us begin anew." She was smiling, which Horace took as a favorable omen. The two of them sat on the deck, drinking coffee, until Beatrix abruptly announced she wanted to return to Miss Nason's house. "I believe there are more secrets to be revealed. The others can join us later at the house. Shall we leave a message and enjoy a morning walk?"

They were a block from Miss Nason's home when Fred and Theo and Clarice drove past, cheerfully waving. "I am glad they didn't offer us a ride," Horace said. Beatrix's head was down, and he didn't see her smile.

"Well, it's easy enough to see how the shelving came down on her," Horace said, once he joined his brother in the yarn room. "Take a look at this, Theo, would you? She had two units stacked on top of each other, so it was top-heavy. That explains why it came down on her."

"You're right about that. It probably wouldn't have happened if she'd fastened them together. Metal strap on the outside, or even nailed together. Too bad. We know how it happened, but the unanswered question remains as to why it happened, what caused it, or who caused it. You think maybe she tried getting something off the top half and the whole unit started to wobble? You know, lost her balance or something, grabbed the shelf, and it came down," Theo said carefully and slowly, thinking his way through the mystery.

"Alright. That's a real possibility. But, then the question becomes what was up there that was so important she didn't get a ladder or even a chair? What could have been so valuable that it caused her to panic and rush? The only thing I see that she kept in here were skeins of yarn and knitting needles."

"Maybe it was a priceless skein of yarn," Theo suggested, then added, "but I've never heard of a priceless yarn, have you?"

"Not my area of expertise. Maybe Clarice would know something. Try asking her. It could be its value was sentimental. You know, first skein she ever bought, or one that somebody important gave her. She is so methodical maybe she kept it as some sort of a memento. Things like that. Everyone keeps saying that Fairy Nightshade collected yarn. Maybe it was something given to her by someone special, or, oh, who knows? Look, let's go through this mess and see if something jumps out at us."

"Such as?" Theo countered. "Collected? That woman was a yarn hoarder!"

"I don't have the slightest idea, but we might get lucky." Horace bent to pick up several skeins, looking at them one at a time. He was about to add that they should try thinking like Beatrix, but thought better of it.

"Stop! What are you doing? Stop it, immediately!" Beatrix demanded as she stood in the doorway.

"Just tidying up a little," Theo answered.

"Please do not do that. This room may contain some valuable clues."

"It's just this yarn on the floor," Theo objected. "We were putting it away so we wouldn't walk all over it."

"And that might be the clue. Perhaps it is the way it fell on the floor, the pattern, but more likely, something important is missing." Beatrix came into the room, careful to avoid stepping or brushing against anything on the floor. "It could be the way it spilled onto the floor, or something else," she said softly, repeating almost as if it were to herself. For a few silent minutes she examined the opposite shelf, searching as always, for connections and patterns. Then she smiled, knowing she had found it. Miss Nason had organized everything according to color and thickness, each skein carefully added to a stack of others similar to it, a space of two inches, and then another color.

"Doctors, would you put the bottom case back against the wall, out three inches?" Beatrix watched as they completed the task. "And now, I will help you lift the top part back into position. I am sure it is far heavier than it appears. You will lift; I will steady and supervise the positioning." Horace and Theo looked at each other and got on with the task. "Now, this is interesting," she commented once they had it back in place. "Horace, Theo, if you look at the front of the sides you will see it is not even. The wood is not cut square, which creates wobbles. That may explain how the unit came apart and fell so easily."

Horace stepped over to the side, looking at the area to which Beatrix was pointing. "Recent?" he asked.

"No, unfortunately, well, at least for us. If it were a recent cut, that would be very, very enlightening, proving something malicious was planned. It appears to be quite old. You can see how the wood is dark, so it is not a fresh cut. Perhaps it was out of line when Miss Nason bought it. Considering the appearance of the rest of the house, it might have troubled her at first, and then she forgot about it. Another little piece of the puzzle has been added. We know how it fell, and why. We can now put the yarn back into place."

Theo was puzzled why Beatrix wanted the yarn put into the same perfect piles as the ones on the opposite wall. She meticulously directed them as they put each skein on the shelves. When she was finally satisfied with the appearance, she stepped back to look at their work. "Much better," she said quietly.

"And another clue?" Theo asked.

"No, not at all. It is tidied up again. And, it demonstrates that a man is as perfectly capable in cleaning, sometimes, as a woman," she answered blankly, turned on her heels and left the room. Theo looked at her, his mouth open, astounded that she would have them go through all that effort just to straighten up the room for a woman who was in the morgue with her next stop the cemetery. He realized it was her revenge for his comments the night before.

"Did you find what you were looking for?" Clarice asked.

"No," she said flatly. "I believe Horace and I should walk back." Beatrix led them out of the house. "It will give us time to think before we begin exploring the treasures in the boxes."

"Assuming that there are treasures in there," Horace countered. "Well, let's walk back and get started," he said without enthusiasm.

"The boxes are in chronological order. At least, Miss Nason made that easy for us by dating them. All we have to do is go through them and find the clues," Beatrix said brightly.

Horace groaned as he, Fred, and Theo stood in front of the stack.

"Is there some real purpose to this work, or do you just want to make them neat, nice, and tidy?" Theo snarled. Beatrix ignored both of them.

"One more thing, please, Fred. I am sure that by now our Doctor Landis will have released the body and arrangements are being made for her burial. It would be very helpful if we could find out when and where the services are to be held." Beatrix nodded toward the library door, indicating he should be on his way. "You could find out from Mr. McVea the undertaker, but I suggest you go to a cafe and learn additional information from your fellow coffee drinkers."

"Where do you want us to start? With the oldest, or start at the newest and work our way back?" Horace asked once Fred was out the door and Theo had followed behind him.

"Oldest. We'll work together on each box. That way one of us might spot something important that the other misses."

Fred ambled over to the Green Parrot Cafe to start inquiring about the services, taking his time so that he could delay his return and what he was sure would be more work. He was also certain that the coffee drinkers and donut dunkers would already know the details and more. Whether their information would be accurate was always another matter. One of the fellows at the table laughed and said, "Better be the biggest church they can find. Half the town will be there just to be sure she's really dead!" The others laughed in agreement.

Without waiting for an invitation Fred pulled up a chair to join them, then waved at the waitress for a cup of coffee. "That well liked, huh?" he asked. He hoped his interest and open-ended question would start the conversation.

"No," one of the fellows snorted. "The wife couldn't stand her, and she weren't the only one. No one could. That old biddy was always strutting around, poking her nose in everyone's business and telling them what to do."

Two others nodded in agreement. "She was a right piece of work," the waitress said as she put Fred's coffee on the table, sloshing a little of it into the saucer. "She'd come in here and tell me how to do my job. You know, smile more, stand up straight, that sort of thing.

A couple of days ago she dinged me out of my tip because I didn't smile enough to satisfy her, and it wasn't the first time, either. I'm glad she'd dead. I shouldn't say it, but there, I did! I'm glad she is dead!"

Fred watched as one man at the table, and then another, reached for his billfold, extracted a dollar bill, and put it in the center of the table. "That shouldn't have happened to you, Cassie," a fellow said softly. The others in the cafe agreed, three of them at the next table putting some money on a saucer then passing it to Fred's table. "She was a real piece of work, wasn't she?" one of them asked.

"So, what else did she do?"

The man some of the others were calling Joe, snorted. "What didn't she do? That's more the question. That woman must have stayed up all night just figuring out ways to make everyone miserable. I'll tell you what she did. I used to deliver coal until my leg stove up, and if I was anywhere on her block, you'd see her hiding behind her front window lace curtains, watching. I could see them twitching, so I knew she was there. About the time I was finishing up, she'd come out that front door of hers and tell me that I should be working faster, or that I'd parked on the lawn and ought to know better. Things like that. And then before I could get back to the office, she would call my boss to complain I'd dropped a piece of coal on the ground. Things like that, all the time. At least he was on to her and told me to forget about it."

Another fellow cut in. "My boy was a soda jerk down to Parrish's, and she'd come here to see who was sitting at the counter. I'll tell you, if they were from around here, they skedaddled out the door real quick. One time, she came in and told Cal he wasn't scooping ice crème the right way because he was using his left hand instead of his right. Gave him a big lecture about it, too. Can you believe it?" He looked towards the counter and watched as Cassie went into the kitchen. Leaning closer so she couldn't hear him, he said, "Bad enough she did it to Cal, but Cassie's hard put ever since her man died, and with an ankle-biter and all."

Fred was getting the general idea that Fairy Nightshade's nickname was well deserved, and if he didn't change the subject, the conversation would circle around and around for hours. "So, anyone know when she's getting buried? Seems like it might be interesting to be there."

"I heard that Reverend Didirot is doing the job. He's a retired pulpit pounder who helps out once in awhile when the regular preacher in town is sick or on a summer vacation. Came up years ago for the Chautauqua and comes back every year. Say, I heard that the women aren't too pleased about it because they'll have a big crowd and there isn't no family to pick up the tab. And besides, she didn't rightly belong to any church, so it's likely to be a graveside service and that's it. Anyone else, they'd go all out for 'em in a heartbeat, but they sure don't like it this time. Not for her," the man behind the counter told them. "I hear it's at one o'clock tomorrow afternoon. Say, you think someone's going to put a stake through her heart like they do a vampire so she won't come back from the dead to haunt us?" He laughed at his own macabre joke.

"Naw," Joe said. "Doc Landis probably couldn't find one. But I hope they embalm her real good."

Fred had his information; he finished his coffee, then got up to leave. "Guess I'll see you fellows back here again tomorrow, seeing as how they won't have eats afterwards." He turned at the door to give a final wave in their general direction as one of them shouted, "Don't count on getting fed." The others laughed.

With Fred off on his assignment, and with Beatrix and Horace buried in the slow task of sorting through Fairy Nightshade's documents, Theo was left to his own devices. "I know what Horace means about being in the waiting room," he told himself. For a long time he leaned on the rail of the Aurora, looking out over the pleasure boats and canoes going up and down the river. Even though he would not admit it, he was bored. The water mesmerized him, and he began wondering if Horace was also bored, and perhaps that was why he enjoyed Beatrix's company. The idea of them together still made him shudder, but it made logical sense to him. "Well, maybe that's the reason they put up with each other."

Theo lost track of time leaning on the rail, and was caught by surprise when Phoebe came up to him. "Look what Aunt Clarice bought me. My own knitting sticks! They're number tens!" she said, holding them up to show him. "She's going to take me to a knitting group in a few minutes."

"Fascinating. So this summer you're going to learn how to knit?" he asked. "I like the way you do something new every summer. A couple of years ago it was learning the Morse Code, and then it was playing the piano. This year it's knitting."

"Well, maybe," she said slowly. "But I thought that if I went with Aunt Clarice I could be Grandfather's spy at the same time. After all, Miss Nason was a knitter, and the women all knit, so I might learn something important to tell him so you can solve the case. Perhaps even a real clue!"

"Wonderful! That's perfect. I didn't know Clarice was going to a knitting party today. By the way, I think she calls them needles; knitting needles, not sticks."

"I know, Uncle Theo," she said brightly. "Maybe. But they look like sticks to me. Got to go. Aunt Clarice is waiting for me." She gave him a quick hug and ran off to join Clarice who was standing at the edge of the gangplank.

"Bring back some news!" he called after her.

CHAPTER TEN

It was mid afternoon before Beatrix and Horace stepped out of the library and on the deck to stretch and get the circulation back into their limbs and brains. "Well, what have you found so far?" Theo asked as they walked over to where he was sitting.

Beatrix sat down hard in one of the deck chairs, drained, her eyes red from reading for hours. "I believe she was a very unlikeable woman," she yawned. "I found out that she taught home economics classes in a high school in Elgin...."

"That would explain all the yarn, then," Theo said. "And, how she became a teacher when she moved here during the war."

"Yes. Yes, I believe so, although she did seem to have an excessive amount of yarn. It might have been explainable if she was planning on teaching knitting here, but Clarice said that the woman in a shop here in town said she lost her best customer when Miss Nason died. There was nothing said about her teaching her students or anyone how to knit. That could mean she was obsessed with buying and storing yarn for some peculiar reason."

"Anything else?" Theo asked.

"Just that she was utterly despicable," Horace added, merely repeating what they all knew.

"Yes. So far I have found two unusual things," Beatrix continued before Horace could say anything more. "The first is that she makes mention of a sister."

"I wonder if she is still alive and knows that her sister died?" Theo asked. Beatrix responded with a blank look on her face. "What's the second thing?"

"She was meticulous about keeping records of everything. Well, more accurately, everything about everyone. Nearly all of it was critical. The minister at a church needing a haircut. A woman on the street whose ankles were visible. Food, clothing, you name it. And, I mean a daily record in her diary," Beatrix said. "I found it mentally exhausting just reading all of the daily entries, and they are repetitive."

"As I said, a despicable woman," Horace repeated.

"Well, that does seem strange. A lot of people are like that, but they don't keep lists in a diary. Anything to do with yarn?" Theo asked.

"In her diaries she lists the prize money and ribbons she won for her knitting, but not what she knitted. Just a list of ribbons and money. The other point that is missing is where she won the prizes."

"You're right, that is odd," Theo said quietly. "It seems to me it's the ribbons that matter more than a few cents. Do you two remember old Mr. Bigelow and the ribbons he won at the county fairs for his produce? I don't think the Fair Board ever paid more than a quarter, but they gave out ribbons for every entrant and every entry. He used to string them up from the ceiling in his front parlor for everyone to see. Some of them were so old and dusty you couldn't tell if he came in first or last. You remember, if he got started, how he'd say where he won each ribbon. But our Miss Nightshade only records the money and ribbons."

"I agree. What I find strange are notations for relatively small amounts of money she received. There are no names or explanations. And, that is unusual because she was very thorough on everything else," Beatrix told him.

The three sat in silence, staring at each other, trying to find an explanation. "Well, if she won awards for her knitting, maybe she sold some of her pieces?" Horace suggested.

"I hope it is that simple," Beatrix answered.

"And, probably more boxes to examine?" Theo asked.

Horace and Beatrix nodded in silent agreement.

"Have you found all these ribbons yet?" Theo asked.

"I may be completely wrong, but she kept all of that yarn where she could see it. She hoarded the stuff. I do not believe she would put the ribbons away from where she could easily look at them and touch them. I believe they were in the yarn room," Beatrix said firmly.

"Maybe she didn't care about the ribbons. Or, maybe they were stolen? Perhaps by the murderer?" Horace asked, leaning closer and barely whispering. "I can't imagine someone killing another person over a handful of ribbons."

"Neither can I. But do you remember pointing out those tiny threads on the frying pan?" Beatrix asked.

"Yes."

"What if the murderer took the ribbons and burned them as an act of revenge?"

"All right. But how does that explain the red phosphorous traces you found?" he asked.

"A fire that hot would have burned all traces of them. I was fortunate to find even just those few threads."

Horace sat back and thought it through. "That would be diabolical," he said, blowing the air out of his cheeks. "Thunderation! To destroy someone's life's work, like that?"

"It would be an act of revenge," Beatrix said slowly, letting her words sink in. "Revenge and pure hatred. And furious anger." All Horace could do was shake his head in horror at such an act.

Finally, Horace asked, "Now what do we do?"

Beatrix looked at him and gave a wintery smile. "I don't know what you are going to do, but I'm going to do exactly what any forensic pathologist would do – search for more evidence; for something we might have missed."

Horace looked at her and smiled. "Good answer."

"You're welcome to assist," she said quietly, and added, "Come along, Sherlock...." when he didn't move out of his chair.

"In a minute. Theo, is Fred back yet?" Horace asked his brother.

"Back and gone out again. He got the lowdown on the plans for the funeral tomorrow. And, he told me that the Odd Fellows have their lodge meeting tonight. He's going to see if some of his lodge brothers might have a few things to say about Miss Nason."

"Good news. It's a good plan," Horace said, groaning, as he got up out of the chair to return to the library. He paused at the door. "Let's just hope he finds out something new. So far, we've had one theme and endless variations."

"Grandfather, you and Doctor Howell look tired," Phoebe said after she came into the library and sat next to him. "What are you doing?"

"Oh, a lot of reading. Doctor Howell and I are working our way through all the boxes of books, looking for clues."

"Did you find any?" she asked brightly.

"No, not yet. How about you sitting quietly for a few minutes while we finish this box, if you don't mind; then I want to hear about your day over dinner."

"Okay." She sat down, turning the chair so she could look at the boxes stacked along the wall. "Grandfather, why does that box have numbers that look different? There is a curve at the top of the two number ones."

"I don't know. Which year?"

"It's from 1919."

"Maybe she was just being creative," he answered, trying to remain focused on the work in front of him.

"What did you just say, Phoebe?" Beatrix asked. "Something about curves on the top of the numbers?"

The girl repeated almost word for word, what she had said to her grandfather, pointing at the boxes, and was surprised when Beatrix's mouth fell open.

"I didn't notice that! Oh! Serifs!" she moaned. "Horace, we must look in the 1919 box! How did we miss the anomaly?" She wheeled around in her chair, watching Horace lift off several other boxes in the stack to get it. He brought it over to the table, and they opened it.

"Doesn't look like anything different to me. Books, notebooks, same as the others," Horace said. "Maybe she was just using a different style that year," he told Beatrix.

She lifted out one of the books to open it. Her eyes widened. "She was definitely being creative," she barely whispered. Horace saw what she meant. The cover was like any other cover, but the inside body of the book had been hollowed out. Both of them were dazed to silence. She closed it quickly and put it back in the box.

"Grandfather, what is it?" Phoebe asked.

Horace swallowed hard, still staring at the books in the 1919 box, and quietly said, "Would you ask your Uncle Theo and Fred to step in here, please."

CHAPTER ELEVEN

"Come in and close the door, would you?" Horace said to his brother and Fred before he turned to his granddaughter. "Phoebs, how about if you tell me all about your knitting adventures in a few minutes. Jake with you?"

"Jake," she said reluctantly and left the library, pulling the door closed behind her.

"What have you two got yourselves into this time?" Theo asked. His eyes widened when Beatrix opened one of the books. He could barely whisper, "It's hollowed out, and packed full of money!"

"Hollowed out and full of money. There is three hundred forty-two dollars in this book alone. From what we have seen so far, the rest of them are the same. All of them are hollowed out and filled with bills," Beatrix told Theo and Fred. "We have not yet counted it."

"Guess I know who's going to spring for a Green River this evening," Fred chortled.

"That would be stealing! The money is not ours. I am sure you realize that," Beatrix said sharply.

"Yeah, I know. Just having a little fun. Course it's not ours to keep," Fred said, trying to mollify her.

"Any idea how much is there?" Theo asked.

"Not yet. We opened the first book and found money, then looked at the rest of them. That's when we called you two," Horace explained.

"I don't know what to say," Theo said quietly.

"I believe we should send for Captain Garrison. This is not our money," Beatrix told them.

"I agree. But it's a matter of timing. First, we don't know the total amount. And second, we need to think this through before we do anything and get ahead of ourselves," Horace told them. "If we have Garrison come over here now, he'll take the money, and so he should. He told us to solve the case one way or another, and we're still looking for clues right now. I think we should wait, sit tight, as they say, for a while longer. We need to figure out where she got all this money, and how."

"He may accuse us of stealing some of the money," Beatrix objected.

"I agree. He might do that, but I still think Horace is right. We wait a while longer. Besides, knowing the way Garrison behaves, even if he were here when we opened the box, he could just as easily say that we took some of it back at Miss Nason's house," Theo added. "Let's see how much more is in there first."

When the last book had been opened and the money counted, it came to over eight thousand dollars. "That's a lot of money," Theo whistled. "She probably didn't trust banks, and that's where she kept it. A lot of people were like that. Our folks never trusted a bank since the one back home failed. Some old-stagers still are that way now. So, what do we do with it now?"

"Is it safe for us to keep it here?" Beatrix asked.

"What are you thinking?" Horace asked.

"I am sure everyone knows, or will soon know, that we are working with Chief Garrison, and that we took all of these boxes. Anyone could have seen us do it. If they know about the money, if they even suspect there was even a small portion of this money, they will come here. Our cabins will be the first place they may look," she answered.

"How about I hide it behind Doctor Howell's science experiment?" Fred offered. The others readily agreed, with Theo suggesting that he slip down to the engine room without anyone seeing him.

"Perhaps the best time would be right after Mrs. Garwood rings the first gong for dinner. Everyone will be moving around and getting eager to sit down to the table," Beatrix suggested. "Wrap it up in some butcher's paper, then put it in a paper bag and tie it up. I am sure there must be some paper and string in the galley."

Fred was the last to join them for dinner. He smiled, and ran a finger across the right side of his nose. The deed was done, and Beatrix visibly relaxed.

"You were just going to tell us about your first experience knitting, Phoebe. Sorry we interrupted your plans," Horace smiled.

The girl beamed with excitement. "Well, Aunt Clarice took me to their knitting bee, and showed me how to, well, how to knit!"

"Just the basic simple chain stitch," Clarice hastened to add.

"And how did you do?" Theo asked.

"Well, not so good. Aunt Clarice had gave me a ball of yarn, but I couldn't keep it in my lap like the other ladies. It kept falling off and rolling around on the floor. And once when I went after it, somehow all the stitches I'd done fell off the needles, so I had to start over."

Clarice interrupted. "Why don't you tell your grandfather what you are making, and for whom?"

Phoebe smiled. "I'm knitting a scarf for you, Grandfather! It's purple and orange!"

Horace gulped, and noticed that Beatrix looked down at her plate, trying not to giggle. "Well, if you get good at it, maybe you would like to make another one for Doctor Howell." He felt her sharply tap her shoe against his ankle.

Harriet coughed to get everyone's attention. "To change the subject for a moment: Miss Nason's funeral is tomorrow afternoon. My understanding is that it will be just a graveside service at Riverside Cemetery at one. Will any of you be going?"

"Absolutely," Theo said. "It might be helpful."

"Will the killer be there?" Phoebe gushed.

Harriet was appalled. "Phoebe, it is not polite to use that tone of voice when someone has died! Nor, for that matter, at a dinner table. Paris Manners, remember!"

"Well, the girl is perhaps right," Horace responded. "The killer, that is, if Miss Nason really was killed, might be there."

Beatrix interrupted him. "Often, Phoebe, if there is a suspicious fire, the arsonist makes a point of coming back to watch the fire, and will be found standing at the rear of the crowd. He, and rarely she, wants to see both the fire and the people watching it. So yes, Phoebe you are very perceptive. The murderer might be in attendance. And Harriet, we would find it very helpful if you are there, because you know just about everyone in town. You could point out anyone who is a stranger."

"We are going, aren't we, Mother?" Phoebe asked, still beaming at the praise from Doctor Howell.

Harriet thought for a moment and then nodded. "Yes. And you, young lady, will be expected to remember your Paris Manners."

Fred interrupted, "Say, I've gotta get going, that is if you can get along without me tonight. Big meeting up to the Odd Fellows, and then there's a big feed afterwards. You two docs going to your Masonic meeting?"

"Big feed? You just had your dinner," Mrs. Garwood objected.

"Well, a man can get awfully hungry sitting through those lodge meetings. Now, I can't tell you a lot about what goes on there, seeing as how we took a sacred oath to keep quiet about it, but see, the officers have to march around a little to open the lodge and close it up again at the end, and in between there is all the business to discuss, and so on, so afterwards they got coffee and donuts for the brothers," Fred explained. "And I want to stick around on account of the fact that I might learn something about our Miss Nason. Don't know if the Masons put on a feed, but you might learn something different there."

"Well, it is a good thing you are going to have your 'big feed' because there won't be a lunch after the funeral tomorrow," Mrs. Garwood said, still irritated with Fred.

The three men got up from the table and started down the street. Harriet and Phoebe helped Mrs. Garwood clean up from dinner, and once finished, decided they also would go home. "I have to start out at Ox-Bow in the morning," Harriet explained. She called for Phoebe to join her on the walk home.

To Beatrix's surprise, Clarice came and joined her on the deck. "With all of the activity I feel like I have hardly had a chance to tell you how happy I am to see you again this summer," Clarice said.

"Oh. Thank you," Beatrix answered warily.

"Really, I should be thanking you."

Beatrix turned to look at Clarice, "Why?"

"I know we all grew up in the same town, but I didn't really get to know Horace until Theo first started asking me to walk out with him," Clarice replied. "And I didn't get to know you until high school. What I do know is that the last decade or so has been very hard on him. The war, losing his wife in the Spanish Flu epidemic, and their son being killed. Now, he feels he's being pushed out to pasture by some of the men he brought into the practice. Harriet and Phoebe, and now you, are the true bright spots in his life."

"Harriet and Phoebe are his family," Beatrix objected. "He told me how they reconnected."

"Yes, and that is what makes your friendship with him all the more special in so many ways. I think Horace is very fortunate he met up with you after all these years. I know I am. And, we both know he isn't always easy company." Clarice reached across to squeeze Beatrix's hand. "Thank you for taking him the way he is," she said quietly and firmly. "I'm going to turn in early. There is no telling how late the fellows will be."

Beatrix silently stared out at the water. The conversation had surprised her, and she didn't know what to make of it.

"They certainly do a good job with the ritual. Sharp, precise, and well rehearsed," Theo said as he and Horace walked back from the Masonic Hall. "Nice refreshments, too."

"You know, it has been a long time since I had rhubarb pie. It did taste good, didn't it?" When they got to a street lamp, he paused to pull out his pocket watch, then turned slightly to look at it. "A quarter past nine," he said, closing the watch and slipping it back into his pocket. They walked on and Horace whispered, "We're being followed."

"Yeah, ever since we left the lodge hall. Do we just keep walking?" Theo asked.

"Don't think we have much choice. I don't know if you caught onto it, but I noticed they forgot to put in alleys when they built this town, so at least we aren't going to get blindsided by someone jumping out at us." He decided against telling his brother that it was Beatrix who told him about the lack of alleys.

The sound of the footsteps grew closer, and the brothers turned around to face whoever was behind them.

"We sat in lodge together," the man said, holding out his hand, then giving the Masonic greeting. "You two are investigating the death of Miss Nason, I hear."

"Something like that, yes," Theo said.

The man moved closer to Horace and spoke in barely a whisper. "She is not the widow, daughter, or wife of a Brother Mason, so I am not violating our vows by telling you this, but it must be kept in confidence. Do we agree to meet on the level? She traded in blackmail and extortion."

"And you have something to back that up?" Horace asked.

"I do, but it must be concealed and not revealed. She knew too many secrets, and what she didn't know she made up, and made people pay up. Brothers, among many others. She had her hand out for her money or she threatened to ruin people. Good people. She got a lot of money that way, making people pay up to keep her quiet."

"Without naming names, can you tell us a little more?" Theo asked.

"Well, let's say a fellow hires a new employee, maybe a real looker, and everything stayed on the up and up, but she'd threaten to tell everyone in town that they were stepping out together on the sly if he didn't slip her some money. Or, if a young woman went to the city, she'd tell her folks to hand over some money or she'd say that the girl left on account of her being in the family way, if you brothers get my meaning. Things like that. She knew how to ruin people."

"How did she get away with it?" Horace asked.

"She had some real dirt on a couple of people, just enough to make everyone scared, and after that, it was easy. She'd tell the folks who had secrets to hand it over or she'd have a little talk with someone else – or worse. She got them to do her bidding and she got their money. A lot of it."

"Quite the busy little lady," Theo said.

"She was no lady, not by a long shot," the man replied.

"No, obviously not. You've been helpful."

"A brother's duty to a brother. Wait here and count to ten, and do not try to follow me. That is all I ask."

"Agreed," the brothers said in unison.

"We met on the level and now we depart upon the square," he said, stepping back into the shadows.

"Well, that was interesting," Theo said when they resumed their walk home. "You think he was being straight with us?"

"Certainly sounded like it to me. Did you hear that slight quaver in his voice when he spoke about extortion and blackmail? My guess is that he knows firsthand what he's talking about. And probably knows a lot more from others."

"Makes me wonder if one of the members took care of business," Theo said slowly and quietly.

"I don't like to think about that, but you might be right," Horace answered.

Theo let out a soft whistle. "I'm starting to think you and Beatrix might be onto something. She thought it was murder right from the start, but I sure didn't see it. What that fellow just said explains a lot, doesn't it? You know Horace, your Beatrix, now she's got brains. I'll have to admit it, even if I can't figure her out."

CHAPTER TWELVE

As a growing number of people waited for the hearse to come down the drive at the cemetery there had been a little grumbling about the lack of refreshments. "Not so much as a slap of ham in a bun and a pickle on the side," one of the men Fred had met the day before at the diner told his companions. One of his friends reached over and patted his bulging midsection and said, "Looks like you've been to too many funerals as it is," and the others with him laughed.

"Fred," Horace whispered, "I'd like you to slip around over there to the other side of the crowd. Scout out the territory and keep your eyes open for anything that looks suspicious."

"Yes, Sir, General. Just what are you thinking might be suspicious?"

"Well, something out of the ordinary, somebody trying to hang back, but they're watching the burial but don't want to be noticed or talk to anyone. I can't tell you anything better than that. Just keep watch and, well, keep watch."

"Yes, Sir, but it sure would be a lot more helpful if I knew what I was looking for," he answered. "It sure was a lot easier over there in France when everybody was in a uniform."

"Not now, Fred. Pay special attention to anyone standing alone, especially if they are near the back of the crowd. And anyone who leaves quickly once the service is over," Beatrix added. "If it is possible, make eye contact with them."

Fred nodded and wandered over to the opposite side of the crowd.

"There are a lot of people here," Harriet said. "More than you would have expected for someone people despised so much." They watched as the hearse drove past them, and Horace and Theo removed their hats in silent tribute. Six men stepped forward to carry the coffin, and at a nod from the undertaker, Reverend Didirot began. The rain, which had been threatening all morning, started to come down in a soft drizzle. A sea of black umbrellas unfurled and went up, blocking their view of the crowd.

"We are too far away to hear anything," Theo observed.

"We are here to observe," Beatrix whispered back to him. "Watch for anything unusual, or anyone acting differently from the others."

For a moment Theo amused himself with the idea that maybe he should be watching Beatrix, then focused on the crowd. Like Fred, he had no idea what he should watch for, nor whom he should watch during the short service. After the casket was lowered into the ground and Reverend Didirot said a short prayer, the crowd was dismissed, many of them left in a hurry, eager to get out of the damp weather.

"You ready to go?" Theo asked.

"No. Go ahead. We'll walk back in a little while," Horace told him. "You and the others get out of the rain. Anyway, Harriet has to get back to Ox-Bow. Tell Phoebe she's welcome to stay with us. Beatrix looked up at him in surprise. "We might learn something," he whispered to her.

Horace and Beatrix wandered through the cemetery, pretending to look at the headstones, all the while keeping an eye on Miss Nason's gravesite. Reverend Didirot had talked with a few people, then left. Several cemetery employees who had been waiting to one side, trying to stay out of the rain under an oak, began shuffling a bit closer, their shovels in hand. On a couple of the gravel roads, a few people were lingering next to their cars, talking and then leaving. The crowd was all but gone just as the drizzle stopped. "Now, maybe we'll learn something important," Horace whispered to Beatrix.

"What are you expecting?" she asked.

"I'm not certain. A lot of the people who came were just curious or thought they had a duty to a neighbor to be here. I'd say most of them are gone by now. It's the last ones who leave who can be the most interesting. They hang around because something is on their mind."

"I see," she said. They continued slowly walking among the tombstones. It made Horace smile. Beatrix was a whiz in a laboratory, but she never would have received high marks for her bedside manner.

They watched as the gardeners finished filling in the grave and got back into their truck. No one else remained, and Horace suggested it was time to leave. "Not yet," Beatrix whispered. "Over there," she pointed to some pines at the far end of the cemetery. "Someone in dark clothes. You were right about staying."

They moved behind a larger oak to wait and watch as the person stepped out onto the grass, looked around, and walked quickly to Miss Nason's grave. The visitor paused, barely long enough to drop a single red rose on the newly turned dirt, and hurried away. "Any idea who that is?" Beatrix asked.

"No. Not at all. We're too far away. I couldn't tell if it was a man, woman, or child. Maybe a former student or someone who just felt sorry for an old woman who died. Thunderation, I should have brought my field glasses!"

"We could follow the individual," Beatrix proposed.

"No, let's not. We'd be spotted before we got close. Besides, let's wait another minute and then take a look at that flower the person put on the grave. Maybe there is a card with a name on it, he suggested. They waited and then ambled over, pausing to look at some other tombstones. "It's a single red rose. No card, no message."

"And very little help. None at all. Horace, did you notice it is the only floral tribute here. That is surprising, is it not?" Beatrix asked.

"Even for someone so apparently disliked, yes. Even her knitting friends didn't do anything. Shall we go back?"

"Yes. I think we should. I saw some motion over at the edge of the graveyard. Do not turn around! We are being watched." Beatrix's voice was anxious.

"Good. That means we might be on to something. Or, someone." They turned around and walked back to the Aurora quietly discussing the funeral.

"You know, I'm beginning to wonder that maybe this isn't a murder or an accident. There is the possibility Miss Nason took her own life," Horace said. "We haven't considered that, you know."

"I do not agree with you," Beatrix replied. "Perhaps we could discuss it over a light lunch. She nodded toward a small cafe.

So, tell me what makes you suggest suicide," Beatrix said when she sat down.

"Several things. First, we know she had lung cancer. Even if she wasn't diagnosed, she must have known that she was seriously ill. Perhaps she made the decision to end it. She wouldn't be the first person to have done it. Second, the one consistent yarn people have been telling us is how despicable a person she was...."

"Horace, please tell me that pun was not intentional," Beatrix said, interrupting him.

"So, maybe she was, I don't know the right word, overwhelmed, by what she had be doing for so long. Remorse? Repentance? Guilty conscience? Something like that."

"It is an interesting idea. Oscar Wilde's Dorian Grey immediately comes to mind. "It is always possible, of course, but for some reason it does not seem likely. I can understand why you are suggesting it, and we will consider it, but the way she died makes suicide seem unlikely. We will keep it in mind, but I believe it is a very weak theory, at least at the moment."

"You are probably right," he said quietly.

"There was something very unusual about that burial," Beatrix said.

"You mean the number of people who came out for someone they all hated?"

"No. I am sure some of them came out of curiosity or a sense of duty. There was something else about it. I can not explain it yet."

By the time they returned from their walk back from Riverside Cemetery and the cafe, Phoebe was sitting on the deck under the awning, a ball of yarn in her lap, working on her knitting. "How are you doing?" Horace asked.

"Terrible. I learned how to knit but I can't remember how to purl, and Aunt Clarice isn't here to show me!" she almost wailed.

"Perhaps I can help," Beatrix offered. "May I try?"

"You know how to knit?" the girl asked, her eyes large with surprise.

"Yes. I was your age when my aunt taught me." She sat down next to the girl. "May I?" she asked, holding out a hand to receive the knitting needles. "Let me show you. Remember there are just two basic stitches you need to learn, and a third one later. You have got the first stitch down pat. That is called the 'knit'. See how the yarn goes over every time you make a stitch? Now, the second stitch is the

'purl' and that is where the yarn goes under. And you do it like this."
She showed her several stitches.

Beatrix handed the needles back to her. "You try. Knit once, then
purl once." She watched as Phoebe did it.

"It's hard because it's backward." She objected.

"No, Phoebe. It is not backward, it is reversed. And, it is hard only
until you have done it many times. I am sure you did not get every
letter right the first time you printed or learned the Morse Code.
And, I definitely remember many mistakes when you were learning
to play the piano. This is no different. It only takes practice. May I
show you again?" When she had the needles in her hands, Beatrix
demonstrated the two stitches. "And, in time, you can start knitting
much faster. Want me to show you?

Phoebe's eyes widened as the needles were practically a blur.

"I think Phoebe made a new friend," Clarice whispered to Theo.
She was very pleased; Theo was not impressed.

CHAPTER THIRTEEN

The mile-long walk back into Saugatuck from the cemetery had tired Horace, and made him irritable. "Thunderation! It's the war department!" Horace pointed to Chief Garrison's squad car as it came to a stop and parked along the dock.

"This cannot be good," Beatrix agreed.

"I've been looking for you two," Garrison snapped when they arrived at the boat.

"A beautiful day to go out for a stroll. Say, if you're looking for something to do, I saw a couple of jaywalkers when we crossed Butler Street," Horace told him.

"I'm not interested in any jaywalkers, and the mayor don't want me pestering the tourists, or writing them tickets. He says it's not good for business. And I'll tell you another thing that isn't good for business – an unresolved death. You two know anything yet? I just saw Doc Landis and he won't budge on that suspicious death report even if they did give the old lady the deep six today."

"That is because it is still very suspicious," Beatrix said.

"Well, you two doing anything to change that? That's what I want to know," Garrison barked at them. "You made some progress?"

"We have," Horace said with a big smile. "Since you gave us access to the house, we've been going through some of her papers. We're hoping to find a few clues."

"Hoping? You'd better be doing better than just hoping! Well, you're sure taking your own sweet time about it. I could have had it done by now!"

"You know, Beatrix, the chief may have something there. We could hand over the papers and let him deal with it," Horace said as he ran his finger along the side of his nose.

"Yes, that might be an appropriate thing to do. Come with us, Chief," Beatrix smiled as she led the way up the gangplank and into the library. "Please do take all of them. We will even help you carry them out to the car."

"All that stuff? That's not paper. That's boxes of paper! I haven't got time to go through all of that on a chance there might be a clue!" he exploded, pushing his hat back from his forehead. "That would tie me and my men up for weeks."

"Yes, that often happens with investigators, which is why you need to be patient and let us get on with our work. If you are not satisfied with the speed at which we are proceeding, then I believe I speak for Doctor Balfour when I tell you we will resign," Beatrix said firmly. "You may take it all off our hands right now, or you will let us get on with our work."

"No. No, I can see you're working steadily at it. You just keep it up. I'm sure you'll find something and get this resolved. All I want is for you to let me know when you find something out. And, what you find. Soon as you do . That's all. Now, I've got to get back out on patrol," the chief said, backing out of the library door, then scurrying down the gangplank to his car.

"A rat leaving a sinking ship," Horace chuckled quietly to Beatrix. "Don't forget about those jay – walkers," he shouted to the chief as he drove off.

"Yes, and now it is you and me, swamped with paper work. But it was fun while it lasted, was it not?" she smiled.

"Has the all clear sounded?" Theo asked as he came from the stern of the boat.

"It has. And, we have a new wrinkle in our mystery," Horace said. For the next few minutes he and Beatrix told Theo about the mysterious Mr. Wilbur Walker they met at the cemetery.

"That is a mystery," Theo said, rubbing his chin. "The Park House, you said. Well, as soon as Fred gets up from the engine room, we're going to a roadhouse diner south of here. A place called Emma's, Emma Leven's place, I think. We'll stop by the Park House on the way."

"Dare I ask what Fred is doing in the engine room?" Beatrix asked.

"Checking on the progress of your experiment," Theo replied.

"I see," Beatrix said quietly, averting her eyes. "Perhaps, Horace, we should have something light to eat. It will be several hours before the dinner gong."

"How about the Butler? Perhaps some whitefish?" Horace suggested.

"I believe the operative word should be 'light'. I was thinking a piece of pie might be refreshing. We could divide it between us and that way it would not adversely affect our appetites tonight. Or if you do not want something sweet, then perhaps a small salad."

"Right," Horace answered without enthusiasm. "A nice bowl of weeds." He was even more disgruntled when he saw the smug look on his brother's face.

They were about to leave when Mrs. Garwood approached Beatrix. "Doctor Howell: Clarice – that is – Mrs. Balfour, said that when she and Phoebe get back from their knitting party. she's going to the beauty shop to have her hair done. She would like you to go with her."

"That is unusual," Beatrix said warily. "Yes, yes, I will accompany her. We should be back in less than an hour."

"That should be plenty of time," Mrs. Garwood said.

"I keep thinking about that fellow Theo and I met after the lodge meeting last night," Horace said as he and Beatrix awaited for their salad at the restaurant. "I don't think we're going to learn anything talking with people. If Fairy Nightshade has been black-mailing them, then they're going to clam up on us. No one's going to say anything for fear that everyone in this town will collapse like a house of cards."

She nodded and after a long silence added, "And I think one reason Garrison is so eager to get this settled is that he's been one of her victims. That may explain many things. Everyone in this village wants the past buried with her. Their past, in particular. Maybe the right thing to do is simply say we cannot find an answer and leave it at that."

"If we do, then everyone breathes a sigh of relief, and in a few months it will be all but forgotten. Everyone can get on with their lives."

"No, Horace, it won't happen that way. The secrets and distrust will linger and fester. Wounds like that will not heal for years. It may take generations. Sooner or later someone will say something or make an accusation, and then all of it will come pouring out." Beatrix reached a hand across the table, resting it on his wrist, and looked Horace squarely in the eyes. He knew it was an uncomfortable gesture for her to offer. "Horace, you have experienced it." She withdrew her hand and looked down. "So have I," she barely whispered. She did not elaborate, and Horace didn't have the courage to ask.

They finished their lunch, and on the walk home, Beatrix wanted to take his arm, but could not bring herself to do it.

"I am honored that you asked me to accompany you to the hairdresser's, but I am puzzled by the invitation," Beatrix told Clarice on their walk to a shop on Lake Street.

"Because," Clarice said quietly, "I have decided the time has come to bob my hair, and I am counting on you for extra courage if I start to waver."

Beatrix gasped in shock. "Oh! You? I read Francis Scott Fitzgerald's short story "Bernice Bobs Her Hair" several years ago. It was in a magazine. I believe she created quite a few problems for herself. Are you sure this is what you want to do? What will Theo say when he sees you?"

"I'm sure he will have plenty to say, but it is my head and my hair. I'm not doing it for him or to spite him. I've worn my hair the same way since I was Phoebe's age, and I want to change my style. Other women our age have done it. Now, it's my turn."

"It was May 1920, in the Saturday Evening Post. I remember reading it," Beatrix said.

"What was in the Post?" Clarice asked.

"The story I just mentioned. I realize it is dated, but you might want to read it before doing something so drastic. I know it was the May edition, but I cannot remember the page number," she answered. Clarice smiled but did not answer; her mind was made up.

Beatrix gasped again and was a bit shaky when she turned the knob on the beauty shop door. They had barely entered when the receptionist came out to meet them, smiled, and quietly said, "Some of our clients enjoy a little refreshment while they wait, if you know what I mean." She smiled and led them into the back room.

"I'll have one, too," Beatrix said, then remembered to add, "please." Both women giggled as the champagne bubbles tickled their noses. Clarice held up the glass, "Dare you! If I can do it, you can do it. Besides, if you don't like it, you can always let your hair grow back. Come on, let's both of us do it!"

"What if Horace...?" Beatrix started to ask.

"That's the wrong question for a woman who always says she prefers to fly solo. Besides, I think he might have a lot of respect for a woman with a little vinegar and ginger in her. Are you in or out?"

They had finished a second glass when the beautician came into the room to say that she was ready. To Clarice's surprise, Beatrix said, "I'm going first!" There was a silver tray with a filled flute of champagne. Beatrix eagerly reached for it, and swallowed it in a single gulp.

The stylist offered to show Beatrix several photographs, but she smiled and giggled. "Oh, I know the style I want. It is called the Marcel. Parted in the middle and a permanent wave." When the stylist warned her that sometimes it can be a bit frizzy, especially on damp days, she smiled again, "Good. Let us hope so."

"And Madame?" another stylist asked Clarice. "Oh, make me look like Theda Bara," Clarice responded. "Or is it Clara Bow who is the Vamp? I never can remember. Smooth shaped, bangs, and spit curl near the ears. We'll see if my husband notices."

"Trust me, Madame, your husband will most definitely notice!"

"What if he does not approve?" Clarice asked.

Beatrix giggled. "Tell him it was my idea and I talked you into it."

"I may have to hold you to that. I'll tell you what. If Horace squawks about it I'll tell him you bobbed your hair because you think he looks like Valentino and wanted to keep up with him," Clarice said with a sly smile.

Beatrix gasped. "No! You must not do that! I have never said such a thing! He might get the wrong idea."

"Well, that was a fool's errand," Theo said when he and Fred returned and joined Horace in his library. "No one by the name of Nason or Walker at the Park House. No record of anyone from Peoria in the registration book or the telephone log book. And no record of any calls from anywhere in town to Peoria."

"I am not surprised," Horace said. "He's probably not using his real name."

"That's what we thought, too," Theo said. "Which is why we checked at the telephone office. We couldn't find any place else so ended up at the Green Parrot. Nothing. In fact, we were the only ones there. So, we've struck out on both accounts. We're running out of possibilities."

"That's what I want to tell you docs about," Fred replied. "You know how I went down to check on the experiment Doctor Howell's doing? Well, it's still there, perking right along, and say, it's a good thing it's down there. And I figured that while I was there I ought to check to be sure the money is still there, which I done did and which it is.

"And then I got to thinking about a couple of years back out to Ox-Bow when we had that dust up with those fellows making phony bonds. You remember? Well, it occurred to me that maybe this money we found the other day might be phony, too. So, I took a bill out and held it up to the light, and there was this writing on the top that's invisible unless you look for it the right way. Here, I brought some of the stuff along with me. I was going to tell you earlier, but Doc Theo wanted to get over to the Park House, and you and your lady friend were going out for lunch, so I figured it could wait a little while longer."

When he pulled two bills out of his pocket, Horace and Theo both reached for them. "Up there along the top over on the left side. You see those numbers?" Both men did. "Now, you look in the middle and there's some more writing. You see it? You got to hold it up to the light just right."

"I've got eight numbers," Horace said. "What about you, Theo?"

"Letters that don't make any sense. Looks like an eye chart. Fred, are all the bills like this?"

"I don't know. I found those two to show you and then we got busy until now."

"Fred, please go down and bring up all the money," Horace said quietly. As soon as Fred was out the door, Horace asked his brother, "You have any ideas?"

"Not a single one. That old lady was crazier than I thought possible."

"Crazy or crazy like a fox. I don't know which," Horace answered.

Half an hour later, when the three men had looked at almost every bill, finding them all marked with invisible ink, they looked at each other, shaking their heads in disbelief. "It has to mean something," Horace said, "but for the life of me, I can't figure it out."

"I'd say we have a code to crack," Theo yawned wearily. "I can see a pattern to it, but I have no idea what it means. You know, I have a feeling that Beatrix is the one for this mystery."

It was just about that very moment, for the first and only time in her life, that Mrs. Garwood dropped a metal tray. It was the unexpected and shocking surprise of seeing Beatrix and Clarice coming up the gangplank after their visit to the beauty shop, both of them slightly unsteady on their feet. At first Mrs. Garwood thought they were guests or day-trippers who walked onto the wrong boat, but after a second look she recognized them and promptly dropped the tray.

The racket sent Horace and Theo out of the library, with Fred given firm instructions to guard the money in case it was a robbery. The brothers had barely stepped out onto the deck when Clarice cautioned, "I would think very carefully before you say anything, dear." It was needless advice. Horace and Theo were stunned to silence as they stared at the women.

"I think," Horace said very slowly and softly, "this calls for a toast to two very courageous and charming women."

"Very nicely done, Horace," Beatrix said to him with a rare smile, then looked away for a moment and added "Thank you."

To shatter the last of the tension, Horace called for Fred to join them on the deck. "Couple of ladies want to meet you!"

"Say, you two look swell. A couple of real high society dames," he said. "Real swell."

"Fellows, we've got to change our plans," Horace said.

"I thought we were going to see if we could break the code once Beatrix got back," Theo countered.

"We were, but Clarice and Beatrix changed everything. Now look, that money will wait until tomorrow morning. Fred, store it away for us again back where you keep it. Theo, your Clarice was probably worried sick about how you would take it if she changed her hair, she probably did it for you. I think we ought to go over to the Big Pavilion and do something special. Give them a boost of confidence or something," Horace said.

"Did you ever think maybe it was Beatrix that came up with the idea, hoping to get your attention, and got Clarice to go along with it?" his brother asked.

"Beatrix? I doubt it. Besides, I'm sure she knows I appreciate her. She has a brilliant mind. All I'm saying is we should to make this a special evening."

Theo shook his head, wondering how his brother could be so clueless.

CHAPTER FOURTEEN

Mrs. Garwood said very little when she served dinner that evening, and didn't dare look at Clarice and Beatrix for fear that disapproval might show on her face. The captain, standing in the doorway of the galley, kept staring at them. From the way he smiled when he was certain his wife wasn't watching, he definitely approved of their change to a modern style.

It was, surprisingly, Harriet who put a damper on their dinner that evening. She looked at Beatrix, then at Clarice, and back at Beatrix again, before averting her eyes and saying almost nothing during the entire meal. It was obvious that she did not approve of their hairstyles. Her iciness was noticeable, and it fell to Horace to change the mood.

"So, Phoebs, how did the knitting go this afternoon?" he asked his granddaughter.

Her eyes brightened. "Wonderfully. Thanks to Beatrix, I mean, Doctor Howell, helping me this morning; I could knit and purl, and I learned that you can knit one and purl one, or knit one and do several purls, or several purls and several knits or just one knit. It all depends on the pattern and keeping count. It's fun! Grandfather, maybe you can take me shopping for some more yarn."

"Well, that seems like it might be a fun outing. Now, did you learn anything else?"

"Scads! Several of the women were telling things they remembered about Miss Nason, and..."

Beatrix cut her off. "I apologize for interrupting, but could you tell me if Miss Lee, the woman they call the Mouse, was present?"

"No. No, I'm sure she wasn't," she said curiously

"Nor was she at the funeral. Horace, do you remember me saying that there was something odd about the funeral? Now I know what it was: The Mouse wasn't present. She was Miss Nason's closest friend. People say they were always together, and yet she was not at the cemetery. I am very sure about it."

"Maybe she couldn't bring herself to go to it. It wouldn't have been easy for her."

"No, perhaps not," Clarice agreed. "Do you remember when President Roosevelt died, his wife stayed at home and read the burial service alone? Perhaps that's what Miss Lee did."

Beatrix looked at her and said, "That would be unusual. Even I am not that old-fashioned or traditional. We can only hope that her grief was not so severe that she has chosen to do something unfortunate."

The conversation had lapsed again, so Horace tried a new tactic. "Well, we've had a rather busy day, and I think we should celebrate this evening. After all, it's not every day that Clarice and Beatrix step into the twentieth century." He lifted his coffee cup to toast both of them. "I think they ought to have a chance to show off their new hairstyles. Beatrix, what say we go to the Big Pavilion and cut a rug?"

"I do not know that phrase, but the floor there is hard wood. Maybe if Clarice and Theo want to come along," she replied, her head down, almost frightened by the idea.

"Clarice and Theo, Fred, the Garwoods, Harriet and Phoebe. It's a Thursday night so we shouldn't have any trouble getting a table. Fred, do you know who is playing there tonight?" Horace asked.

"No, not off hand. I didn't think to look," Fred answered.

"Doesn't matter. Let's just go, see and be seen, and if we don't like it, we don't have to stay very long. Theo, what do you say? Fred, I know you're game, and so are the Garwoods. Harriet, how about it?"

There was a bit of grumbling and muttering, but in the end she agreed, but only for a short time. She had to go out to Ox-Bow in the morning, and didn't want Phoebe in bed too late.

"Horace, you are up to something, are you not?" Beatrix asked as she and Horace led their group from the boat to the dance hall.

"Yes, and it's not what you think. Over dinner we learned that the Mouse wasn't at the at the cemetery for the funeral. And, while you were out, Theo and Fred reported they couldn't find any trace of our mysterious Mr. Walker. That gave me the idea he might be a grifter. If he is, I won't be surprised if we see him this evening."

"I see. And tell me, just what is a 'grifter'?"

"A con artist, a confidence man. A criminal who is hoping to take advantage of a situation. In a quiet little burg like Saugatuck, there is only one place he is likely to go, unless he is holed up in his room and staying out of sight."

"But if he is not a grifter, then what do you suspect," she asked.

"Probably the worst. Our Mr. Walker might be the killer. Perhaps he killed Fairy Nightshade, hid out of town somewhere for a couple of days, and only pretended to have arrived too late for the funeral. And, since the Mouse was her only real friend, and hasn't been seen since Decoration Day, well, perhaps she's either dead or on ice somewhere. You know: held captive."

Beatrix gasped slightly, then asked, "And this has nothing to do with Clarice and me bobbing our hair?"

"Just the opposite. It has everything to do with your hair. Look, when this fellow saw you yesterday you had long hair. Today, it's bobbed and he isn't going to recognize you at first. When he does, he'll do a very noticeable double-take."

"Oh, I see," she said with a tone of disappointment in her voice. "Then what happens if he is there?"

"I haven't the slightest idea. We'll have to make it up as we go along, assuming he is there," Horace told her.

"Which explains why you have your silver-headed cane with you. Horace, this time, would you mind not getting a gun pointed at us? I really do not want to ruin my new hair-do."

"I think I've heard this before," he said lightly.

"Yes. Yes, you have. And, you never seem to listen."

"Beatrix, a grifter generally doesn't pack heat, you know, carry a gun, that is. I think we're perfectly safe, but if he's something other than a con artist, then I'm taking no chances. Besides, if we do need to get out of there in a hurry, I can always pretend to limp and use the cane as a cover."

"Horace, I question why you believe your sword cane will provide adequate defense against a man packing heat, as you say. I brought along a small calibre equalizer of my own." They continued walking as she opened her handbag to reveal a snub-barrelled twenty-two pistol.

"I am impressed," he smiled.

"I also believe you are quite naive to pin your hopes on one or two individuals. From everything we have learned, every person in this town had very good reason to want Miss Nason dead. They might not be pleased being caught. Committing murder is hard the first time; after that, my observation is that it is much easier. Until there is some advancement in our investigation, we remain in perpetual danger. I hope you will keep that in mind," Beatrix said quietly but firmly.

They found a table near the rear of the Big Pavilion, off to one side. "Perfect location," Horace said. "Fred, across the room, you see those fellows?"

"Yeah, usually if they're going to have some hooch, that's where they sits. Comes in through that little side door over there. I'll bet you want me to keep an eye on them."

"That's right. They're your mark. Join us for a while, and then wander over their direction. And, one other thing, Fred. When we leave, hang back a bit and make sure we aren't jumped from behind."

"You expecting that?" Fred asked.

"I'm not certain what to expect. Nothing about this is any too clear," Horace said. He wasn't ready to tell him about the conversation the previous night after the lodge meeting. Nor was he willing to reveal Beatrix's thoughts a few minutes earlier.

"Don't Aunt Clarice and Doctor Howell look smart with their new hair styles?" Phoebe quietly asked her mother as they sat at their table. Harriet didn't respond. She was watching several couples walk past their table, all of them noticing the two women and smiling in approval.

"Maybe we should get our hair bobbed, too. It's all the latest!" Phoebe tried again.

Her mother turned to her, looked, and cautiously replied, "I'll go all the way to 'maybe'. We'll see. Let me think about it until tomorrow morning. Agreed?"

"Jake with me," Phoebe smiled.

"You know, young lady, you are not helping your cause by resorting to slang. I think your grandfather and Fred are not always the best influence on you."

"Yes, Mother. Agreed. And then tomorrow morning you can say yes."

Harriet wasn't the only one at their table who had noticed the looks of approval. So had Theo, and it wasn't long before he was leading Clarice out to the dance floor, eager to let everyone know he was married to a fashionable woman. "They look like they are having fun," Beatrix told Horace. "I think Theo has recovered from the shock. Have you noticed his posture is different? He is standing much taller – a sign of male pride."

"My little brother isn't the only one who knows how to have fun. Come on, let's cut that rug, like I promised!" Horace said, holding out his hand to take Beatrix out on the floor.

"I do not know how to dance," she objected.

"Neither do a few others, from the looks of things, and it isn't stopping them. I believe the piece the band is playing is called 'Stumbling All Around.'"

Beatrix gulped and got up from the table. By the time they got on the floor, Horace was just as nervous. "Horace," she told him, "this is a fox trot and you are waltzing. You cannot waltz to a fox trot. The tempo is different. You are hopeless on a dance floor, and I am worse!"

"Yes, but I've got the stumbling part down pat," he said, gradually moving them closer to the table at the far end of the room. He turned so that she was facing it. "Anyone look familiar?" he whispered.

"Yes. Mr. Walker is there," she said as he turned her to move with the crowd along the outside of the floor.

"And with some rough looking characters, too. Time to send in Fred," he told her.

"Does that mean we have to sit down, too?" Beatrix asked.

"Absolutely not!" They moved back across the dance floor toward their table, and Horace caught Fred's eye just as the band began playing "Varsity Drag." A nod of the head in the direction of Mr. Walker's table, and Fred was on his feet, ambling over there. To Beatrix's surprise, Harriet and her daughter had gone out on the dance floor, as had the Garwoods.

Horace and Beatrix remained on the dance floor, trying to dance, and intent on watching Fred and Mr. Walker. "Doesn't look like Fred is having much luck," Horace said as he looked over Beatrix's shoulder.

"Do you think he is wary?" she asked.

"I don't know. Maybe there isn't anything funny going on to begin with." Both Horace and Beatrix were relieved when the band took a twenty-minute break and they could return to their tables. Horace had just sat down when he watched Mr. Walker get up and walk out the door. Fred was a few paces behind him, but when Walker got to the door he stopped, turned around, and went back inside. There was nothing Fred could do but continue walking.

"That is ominous. I believe he was very wise in not returning," Beatrix said.

"It would have been a dead give-away that he was tailing him." Horace answered in agreement. "Our Mr. Walker is obviously a professional."

"Do you think he's onto us?" Beatrix whispered.

"I don't know." His voice was worried. "It might be time for us to take a powder." Then, realizing she might not know the meaning, he explained. "Time for us to leave."

At first Beatrix was surprised when Horace didn't escort her on their walk back to the Aurora. She thought he was disappointed in her when she said she wanted to go home. "Too many people; too much noise," she had told him, her face drained of color and her body feeling shaky. He had suggested they leave, but she was certain he was disappointed in her. Only when she saw him waiting for the others to pass, did she begin to understand his plan. He had encouraged Mrs. Garwood to walk with Beatrix at the front of their little procession, while he brought up the rear with the captain. Fred was nowhere to be found, perhaps tailing them at a distance in case they had unwelcome company.

"I figured something was up, what with you wanting to go to the dance hall. I brought along my little friend." The captain partially pulled out a small blackjack from his waistband to show Horace. "And you got that silver headed cane sword. Looks like we're set for anything."

"Beatrix has a little revolver in her handbag. This is one time I'd like to be skunked," Horace chuckled. "Let's shift around a bit. Why don't you move up to the front with your wife and tell Beatrix to fall back because I want to talk with her. Just keep on the lookout when you take the point."

It was a tense walk back to the boat, all the more so with Captain Garwood intentionally sauntering so as to not arouse suspicion.

Horace and Beatrix were sitting in his library long after the others had retired for the night. When Horace told her about the coded messages on Fairy Nightshade's money, Beatrix wanted to immediately begin investigating. "Enough for one day," Horace said. "We'll get to it first thing in the morning. Anyway, I want to know what inspired you to bob your hair."

"I was not inspired. This was Clarice's idea. She wanted to do it. Horace, you must know, until today I always thought the style was, well, slightly disreputable. It is worn by fast women, the sort of women who will dance with a man they do not know, and I do not think it is respectable for a woman my age to indulge in it. I was certain that Theo would feel that way, too, as Clarice is only a few years younger than me. So I went first and dared her to follow me."

Horace's mouth opened. "That way you would take the heat... You know, Beatrix, there is something very..."

Whatever Horace was about to say was interrupted by a light knock at the door, and Clarice's voice asking if she could come in.

"Everything is all right," she said. "Oh, I'm sorry. I didn't mean to interrupt you two."

"You are not, Clarice. Please, join us," Beatrix said.

"Well, I am glad you are both here. With all the excitement this afternoon and then tonight, I haven't had a chance to tell you what I learned at the knitting group."

"What?" both Beatrix and Horace asked together.

"Just this: Fairy Nightshade was not a member of the knitting group. I asked, and they said that her friend Miss Lee, the Mouse, was always there, but Miss Nason never did attend. One of the ladies said she did not think Miss Nason belonged to any knitting circle. I'm not certain, but I think that may be important."

"Did anyone explain why she was not part of the group?" Beatrix asked. "Perhaps she was invited or ordered to leave."

"No, that wasn't it. I played the ditz and asked if she ever did knit, and a couple of women said they had never seen her with knitting needles or yarn. Ever!"

"That is odd," Horace replied.

"Clarice, please tell me that Miss Lee was present today," Beatrix gently demanded.

"No. No she wasn't."

"Oh," Beatrix said softly.

CHAPTER FIFTEEN

Theo was waiting for Horace on the deck early the next morning. "I'm guessing you waited up for Fred to get back here?" he asked.

"Yeah. He got back maybe three-quarters of an hour after we did," Horace told him, trying to stifle a yawn.

"And?"

"We were being tailed all right by our Mr. Walker. Fred stayed back in the shadows and saw him come out a few seconds behind us and follow us all the way to the boat. Then he veered off and took the scenic route back to the Big Pavilion."

"That's interesting," Theo said quietly.

"Fred's good. He trailed behind him, then kept in the shadows and followed behind him back to the dance hall before slipping back here. He said he wasn't followed, and if he said that, then he wasn't."

"For all his quirks, Fred has always been a good man," Theo said. "You think Walker is our killer?"

"Interesting question. I wouldn't be surprised. Everything is pointing in that direction. Fred thought we ought to hoist up the gang plank, but I told him it would be a dead giveaway that we were onto him."

Theo nodded and went to the galley in search of coffee. When he returned, Horace added, "Beatrix and I were talking. The Mouse seems to be missing, and I'm beginning to wonder if she is being held captive somewhere, or maybe she is dead by now."

"That's an interesting twist," Theo said quietly. "The Mouse caught in a deadly trap."

Horace was not amused by the cynical pun.

"It seems to me you're getting in fairly tight with the donut dunkers over at the Green Parrot, and maybe you're about due for a haircut at Dominic's," Horace commented when he saw Fred. "And again, that was a good piece of work last night."

"Long as I don't have to look like some movie star like that Sheik of Araby fellow now that Mrs. Balfour and Doctor Howell have done dolled themselves up. I get your drift: keep snooping around," Fred said with a big smile.

"And before you go, I think we'll need that stash you hid," Horace reminded him.

With the curtains drawn across the library window, the shade removed from the desk lamp, and the doors locked, Horace, Theo, and Beatrix began examining the hidden writing on the money. At first, it appeared almost straightforward. There were numbers written in invisible ink on the upper left corner of each bill, but after that, her system seemed meaningless. They spent the better part of the morning before they could understand Fairy Nightshade's convoluted system and begin dividing up the bills and stacking them on the desk.

"The numbers are a ruse," Theo said quietly. "She numbered them sequentially, but it doesn't mean anything."

"Other than to throw someone off the scent," Horace answered.

"I doubt that was the reason, although it appears to be the result," Beatrix answered.

Theo nodded in agreement. The ones, fives, tens, and twenties have something written with this invisible ink but the larger denominations are blank. Some of them, the ones and fives, have numbers. Then look at the tens. They've got these funny little stick figures on them. All the others, the twenties, fifties and hundreds are blank. This doesn't make any sense," Theo moaned.

"Yes, it does!" Horace exclaimed.

"'The Adventure of the Dancing Men!'" Beatrix clapped her hands in glee. "A substitution code. What an intriguing challenge."

"Dancing men?" Theo asked.

"A short mystery by Arthur Conan Doyle where Sherlock Holmes has to decipher a code. Fascinating! Fairy Nightshade was not only devious, but used Holmes to guide her," Beatrix laughed. "For a woman with a reputation for being so vile, she has one redeeming feature. No, I misspoke. She kept a very tidy house and she read Sherlock Holmes. Two redeeming features."

"All we have to do is watch out for a big vicious dog," Horace chuckled.

"A big dog? What's that about?" Theo growled. "There's been no sign of a dog. And what chemical would she use for invisible ink?"

"Never mind the dog. I can fully explain later. It's a different adventure," Beatrix said. "As for the chemical, the easiest one of all is lemon juice. The ink is easily made now that lemons are so available." She changed the subject and asked, "Who is good at math? We have to work out the formula she used for the numbers and the stick figures."

"Plain geometry," Horace said. "Useless isn't it?" Beatrix nodded in agreement.

"Calculus, if that helps," Theo answered. Beatrix again shook her head.

"You two figure out the ones and fives while I get started on the tens," Beatrix told them.

The sounds of pens scratching on paper, the rustling of the bills, and the ticking of the clock were the only sounds in the library for the rest of the morning. It was only when the noon fire whistle sounded that the trio broke from their work.

"Well, have we gotten anywhere?" Theo asked.

"I think so. Those numbers up at the top are important after all. They aren't to throw us off the scent. We were wrong about that. She numbered all of the ones in sequence, then started over and did the same thing on the fives, and then again on the tens and twenties, and so on. So, if you lay all the ones, fives and tens with the same index number one in a row, there is a message," Horace explained.

"But the twenties on up don't have a second message," Theo objected.

"I believe that part was intended to confuse us," Beatrix answered. "Then again, perhaps she did not have any additional messages."

"On the ones, there are eight numbers. Dates. She used the European style. The first four are the year, the next two the month, and last two are the dates. Once I caught on to it, it was a cake walk. It was what the Allies did during the war, remember Theo?" Horace added. "How did you do with the fives?"

"All numbers, and my guess is that they are the amounts of money she raked in. So, I see what you're saying about those numbers at the top not being useless. The date on the ones goes with the amount on the fives," Theo said. "And that leaves it up to you, Beatrix."

"The ten dollar bills almost look like a laundry list of sin," she replied. "Adultery, petty theft and shoplifting, breaking the prohibition laws, fornication. Plus, swearing and profanity, disobedience to parents, and a few others. My guess is that not even a Catholic priest has heard this many confessions in a lifetime. Oh, and truancy, and some young fellow who was spending too much time reading National Geographic magazines. It becomes a bit repetitious after a while."

"What about the twenties?" Horace asked.

"I will work on that after lunch," she said firmly. "If there are messages on them, I have not yet found them."

"After lunch we'll see if we can find some way it connects to anything," Beatrix sighed. She looked at the clock on the shelf. "Horace, I would be grateful if I could accompany you while you buy a couple of cigars for me." She yawned again.

"Theo, what do you say to stacking up all this money and putting it away for a while? We all need a break," Horace suggested.

"All things considered, we will wait for you on deck to make sure you are not waylaid," Beatrix said. "Then we will go for a walk and cigars."

Once they were well away from the boat and no one was around, Beatrix turned to Horace and said very quietly, "I decoded both the tens and twenties."

"That's good news! Congratulations. But didn't you say there was nothing on the twenties?" Horace asked.

"Well, I was not being forthcoming because I am not certain it is good news," she said, pointing to a bench along the street.

"Why don't you think it is good news?"

"We know the bills are in sequence, and you and Theo decoded the dates and amounts of money. Once I figured out her system and the cipher she was using, I decoded the tens, and then started on the twenties. I am convinced she was a blackmailer, and that may explain why she was killed." She paused to let the news sink in.

"But you just said there wasn't anything on the twenties," Horace objected, still confused.

"Yes, I know. I told you and Theo a direct lie, but I have good reason to think that extenuating circumstances warranted the deception.

"In other words, on this date, this much money, for this reason, and with a name attached. Ones, fives, tens, and twenties. Am I right?"

"Yes." She sat, looking away from him for several minutes. "Do you realize what that means?"

"It means Fairy Nightshade terrorized the village with all of that."

"Horace, it means that if we keep exploring those bills, we will know just as much about everyone as she did. We will know every foible and misstep of everyone here. That is why I stopped after the first two or three. I did not want to know anything more. I believe I had a good reason to deceive you and your brother."

"But you just told me!" Horace objected.

"Horace, you have always proven to be a good man who does the right thing." She turned to look him directly in his eyes. "I trust you and I always feel safe."

Horace swallowed, croaking out a soft "thank you."

"All I ask is that you think about what I have told you. If you believe Theo should be included in this, then I will tell him what I did and why I did it. We are treading on dangerous grounds. I do not mean our personal safety, although that is a risk. We hold the town's secrets in our hands."

"So, for right now, we can stop and say we solved her cipher. It's people, money, and sin. A triple whammy," Horace said quietly. "And from what we've found out, officially, that is, there is enough reason for everyone in town to have had a good reason to bump her off."

"Now what do we do?" Beatrix asked.

"I think we begin by buying your cigars and a couple of boxes of matches for me and then have lunch," Horace replied with a grimace. "We'll let our minds rest and maybe we'll figure out an answer."

"Somehow, we have to get rid of the money, Horace, and I don't believe it can be done locally. If someone happens to discover that invisible writing, it could be horrible. So many people would be hurt, even ruined." Beatrix turned away from Horace so he couldn't see her eyes moistening.

It wasn't until late afternoon that Horace had an idea to which Beatrix agreed. "Basically, it's what you did last year with the paintings and the diaries."

"Smuggling them into Chicago?" she asked.

"Pretty much the same idea."

"It's one thing to take old paintings that might or might not have been genuine, but eight thousand dollars? Horace, that is a lot of money. It could get lost, or stolen, or we could get robbed. Someone might know about it already and follow us out of town. I'm not certain about this."

"I know. I think it's time to send in a bit of extra muscle," he smiled. "We'll see what they say right after dinner."

As always, Fred was enthusiastic about the plan, and Theo was wary. "Theo, it isn't that complicated," Horace explained for the second time. "You, Clarice, and Fred take the morning train into Chicago. You divide up the money, and really, all you have to take are the fives, tens, and twenties, and you go to a couple of banks and tell them you want bigger bills so your wallets won't bulge so much. If you go to different banks the money gets widely distributed in the city over the next few days. And then it gets diluted more widely. You bring the fresh stuff back here, and all the secrets are safe."

"Just a thought, but what if someone at the bank wants to know where we're staying? I don't know why, but to be sure we're not paper-hangers," Fred said.

"People who pass counterfeit money," Horace quickly translated to Beatrix.

Clarice's eyes lit up. "Yes! Fred, you are right! We should plan on checking into a hotel and staying overnight. That way the bank manager could put in a call to the hotel to verify that we are who we say we are."

"Well, if that's the case, then Fred and I can do it without you having to come along, dear," Theo said.

"Oh, I wouldn't dream of it. We can spend the night at the Palmer House, and I'm sure there will be time to do at least a few hours of shopping," Clarice answered. "And in the evening we could have a nice dinner somewhere."

"If we're going to do that, then I was thinking about staying at the Allerton," Theo countered. "There's a new restaurant on the top floor. I think it's the Tip Top Tap."

"Yes dear, but the Palmer House is so much closer to the stores," Clarice reminded him.

"I know," Theo said. "That's why I thought we'd stay at the Allerton. Besides, they have dancing up there."

Clarice ignored her husband, "And Beatrix, I want you to come with me when I go shopping. You don't mind, do you? Besides, if you come along, it will be much more fun. And Horace, you simply must come along as well." She turned to her husband, "I'm sure they dance at the Palmer House, too."

"As much as I appreciate the invitation," Horace answered slowly, "someone has to stay here; and besides, I want to continue going through those diaries. Maybe there is something helpful. Beatrix, I know you've wanted to go through them from the beginning, but if you don't mind I'm going to start with the most recent one and work back."

"I am not certain I approve of your methods, but if you believe it is wise, then by all means do proceed," Beatrix said. Then she suddenly stood up and asked, "Would it be an imposition if Fred drove me out to my aeroplane?"

"Let's not bother Fred," Horace said, reminding her that he still knew how to drive. When they arrived at the airstrip, he assumed that she wanted to check on her plane, and was surprised when she pulled away the canvas cover and asked to put it into the trunk of his car.

She slowly walked around her plane to make sure everything was in good order. "It looks air-worthy, so I am going to take it up. Too much noise and confusion, and too many people. Come with me, Horace!" she called. She laughed and started singing the first lines of "Come Josephine in my Flying Machine" to encourage him.

He looked at her, at the plane, and at Beatrix again. "Why not? he said, pulling himself up and gingerly stepping into the front cockpit.

"You see, you are an experienced air passenger," she said as she waited for him to strap on his leather helmet, and then fastened his safety harness . "One of these days people will be flying all across the country in aeroplanes. Around the world! Good, now you're nicely secured in case I feel like doing a barrel roll or loop!"

"Didn't you forget you need me to throw the propeller?" he asked, hoping to get out of the plane and stay on the ground.

She laughed. "I have a starter motor now. That way I can take off without needing someone on the ground." She turned on the starter, and then the engine. "Ready!"

Once the engine was warmed up, she taxied down the grass strip, turned, and taxied back to where they began to face the wind. Horace could hear the motor racing, and they suddenly lurched at full speed back down the strip and were in the air. Once she had gained altitude, she cut back on the speed and they flew up the Kalamazoo River as far as the swamp and dam near Allegan, then back down again. She pushed the throttle to gain speed, then dropped down low to buzz over Saugatuck and the Big Pavilion before climbing to follow the river down to the lake, and the shoreline down to Macatawa. For the pure fun of it, she circled low over Holland and then went out to the lake again, flying south along the shore to Pier Cove, and finally back to the aerofield.

"You survived!" she laughed once she had taxied back to the near end of the field and turned off the engine. Beatrix looked at Horace and smiled. "You know, I think you had fun! A few more times up in the air with me and you'll understand why it is one of the few times I feel free and light."

"I think I already do," he said. In less than half an hour her attitude had gone from reserved to exuberant.

"Come with us into Chicago tomorrow," Beatrix said once they returned to the Aurora. "It will be much more interesting if you do."

"Perhaps. But I think I should stay here. In case Garrison comes calling, or if our mysterious Mr. Walker turns up, I think I should be around. He's sniffing around like a bloodhound who thinks he's found the scent, and I don't think we should take any chances. And, as I said, I want to continue searching through the diaries. Besides, I distinctly heard Clarice say she wanted to go shopping, and that is not my idea of fun."

He could tell she understood, but knew she was disappointed.

CHAPTER SIXTEEN

Horace was relieved to get his brother's telegram with its terse message, "Work completed; home tomorrow." All had gone according to plan, and without difficulty. He was even more eager for them to return, realizing he truly missed them. The old emptiness of soul, the exhausting loneliness, had returned, and he felt at loose ends all day.

For an hour or so he would work on Fairy Nightshade's diaries with their endless repetitions of the alleged wrongs and mistakes of her neighbors, only to get up and lean on the deck rail, mindlessly looking out across the river. He regretted not going with them and enjoying the fun. His lips tightened when he realized it was Beatrix he missed the most.

It was a little after seven the following evening when he heard a car pull up alongside his boat, followed by the sound of familiar voices. Fred and Theo hurried into Horace's library to greet him.

"I got your telegram. All went well, I take it?" Horace said to his brother.

"Like a walk in the park. I'd say it took about an hour and a half to change all the money. And, before you ask, yes, at different banks. If Fred and I had gone on our own, we could have come back yesterday," Theo said.

"You make better time with fewer people. I take it Clarice and Beatrix went shopping, right?"

"Shopping and the Art Institute," Theo answered wearily.

"And speaking of Clarice and Beatrix, where are they?" Horace wanted to know.

"Putting away their grips. They've got some parcels being delivered here, but I think they have a new outfit they want you to see tonight," Theo replied

"Well, if this is going to become a fashion show, then I'm out of here. I done did see enough of dresses and such in Chicago. I need to check up on my Doctor Howell's experiment, anyway," Fred said, as he hurried out the door. The two brothers continued talking for a few more minutes until there came a knock at the door. Before either of them could say anything, the door flew open and in walked Clarice with Beatrix right behind her.

"Straight from the most fashionable shops in Chicago, wearing the latest style of casual evening clothing for the modern woman, Beatrix Howell," Clarice laughed. She stepped out of the way for a rather hesitant Beatrix to enter.

Between the surprise a day or so earlier when she bobbed her hair, the sight of his friend in blue shirt-waist, light grey linen trousers and a man's jacket to match shocked Horace. Even more surprising was a new white Panama hat. He smiled approvingly. "I never would have thought you so daring!"

"I decided that we have been in mourning for Queen Victoria long enough," Beatrix said. She slowly and awkwardly turned around. "I trust you approve?"

"I certainly do. And it will make it far easier for you to get in and out of that aeroplane! You truly look very smart," Horace said.

"This is not for when I am flying," Beatrix said. "It is for a dinner party."

"And you should see what else she bought," Clarice giggled.

"Clarice! I do not want anyone to see everything you had me purchase!" Beatrix blushed.

For the next half-hour the four of them discussed the trip to Chicago. The money exchange had been the easy part. "By the way, I done did take all that new cash down to where its stashed. And say, that experiment of yours, Doctor Howell, looks like it is percolating along," Fred interrupted when he returned. The rest of the conversation involved shopping and restaurants.

"Oh, and I went down to the sub-basement at the Art Institute to see a colleague," Beatrix said. She paused, looked at the others, and said, "I have been saving this news until we were all together. The preliminary indication is that the two paintings we took down last year are copies. Very good copies, but copies nonetheless. That is only a preliminary analysis. It is not a final verdict, but will keep them all exploring for a long time."

"That's good news. Say, since I didn't know whether your train would be on time or not, I persuaded the Garwoods to take a night off. We're on our own for dinner," Horace told them.

Before anyone else could speak, Clarice said, "Wonderful. You two go ahead, and Theo and I will find someplace on our own. I want him all to myself." She looked at Beatrix and gave her a half-wink. "Beatrix, you are ready to go out for dinner, and Fred, you are truly resourceful all on your own, I'm sure."

"All of you stay right here for a couple of minutes. I'll be right back," Horace said, moving quickly out the door, down the stairs and through the corridor to his cabin. When he returned, he was wearing an off-white linen summer suit and hat to match Beatrix. "Now, I'm ready to go out for dinner!"

"You do not disapprove that I am wearing slacks in public," Beatrix observed as they set off in search of a restaurant.

"Not at all," Horace answered. "Take a look around. A lot of women are wearing them. Trousers, that is."

"Yes, but they are much younger than I, and I still feel a bit scandalous wearing men's clothing."

"Nonsense, you look just fine. Smart, that's the word they use now: Smart. I think you joined the Smart Set."

"Thank you. Clarice persuaded me to buy several new outfits," she said softly.

"I'm glad she did."

She was uncomfortable receiving compliments and quickly changed the subject. "I hope it is acceptable to you that I had them shipped to your boat."

"Oh. Good. We'll keep an eye open for them."

They ordered dinner and, while they waited, Beatrix wanted to know if Horace had found anything useful in Fairy Nightshade's diaries.

"In a word, no. It's just one long repetition about the same topics over and over. You know, we got rid of the money, but we still have all of those boxes of diaries," he told her. "It's not the sort of thing anyone should see."

Beatrix looked down at the table in silence. Even without seeing her face, Horace could tell she was troubled. "I know. At least the messages on the money were in code. This could cause so much pain to so many people," she said quietly. Horace nodded in agreement.

She finally looked up and said, "I had time to think, too. I mentally went through the house, and I know we said we looked everywhere, but we did not. Tomorrow, I believe we need to return to her house once again. There is one more secret."

"Agreed. Beatrix, do you have a compact with you?" he asked quietly and anxiously.

"Yes. Oh, is my....?"

"No, you're just fine. Turn slightly to the right, take out your compact and pretend to be checking your make up. Look over your shoulder behind you."

"At a dinner table? That is never appropriate."

"Be that as it may. Pretend you are checking, and look over your left shoulder behind you. We're being watched."

"By whom?" she asked worriedly.

"Mr. Walker."

"That is probably not good. Now what do we do?"

"I don't see any reason we should interrupt our dinner, especially since it is whitefish," Horace said. "We'll see what he does next. And after dinner... who knows?"

"If he is the legal heir, at least he will not have Fairy Nightshade's money. The original money, that is. I am so relieved it is gone away." Her voice was sad, and after she spoke, she turned away to stare out a window. "Nor do we have to turn over the diaries to him. Legally, of course, they would belong to him, but I propose we say nothing."

"It disturbs you," Horace said, inviting her to respond.

"Yes, all of it. That vile woman snooping on people and then blackmailing them. And then leaving a written record behind. You know what it was, do you not, Horace? It was her sheer gloating over the pain she was causing. More than anything else, I abhor cruelty." She looked at him, tears in her eyes.

"There's been something on my mind since you found the names. It's been troubling me," Horace said slowly.

"Yes, you want to know if Harriet or Phoebe's names were there. That is not being nosy You love them both. Rest assured, they were not on her list. Neither of them. There was nothing about them. I realized when you chose not to accompany us to Chicago, and then you were going to read the most recent diaries, that you were worried about them. That is yet another reason why exchanging the money was so crucial."

"Thank you," Horace answered. "You're right. That money would have created tremendous pain. Maybe that is why you, Theo, and I became physicians. We wanted to take care of those suffering in pain."

She nodded in agreement. "I did. Do you remember the young girl in our second grade class who died of diphtheria?"

"Mildred Van Heusen? Yes, vaguely," he replied.

"I still see her sometimes in my mind. Sometimes she haunts my dreams. Alive as the rest of us on Decoration Day, then dying over the summer. I cannot imagine how her parents ever got recovered. Or, those Civil War soldiers who lost a limb or had part of their face blasted away. Mothers who died in childbirth, parents whose children died, hunger, misery, all of it. Their pain and suffering clings to me. I thought if I became a doctor I could fix things."

"And, we have, Beatrix, we have!" Horace tried to sound cheerful. "We have done our part, done what we could."

"No, Horace. Not I. Having knowledge and medical skills was not sufficient. I had no bedside manner; I did not connect with people. Not like most doctors, and that is what a patient needs as much as a good surgeon. I did not have the ability to be detached and yet compassionate. That is why I became a pathologist. I could hide in my laboratory away from people. Does any of this make the least bit of sense to you?" Her voice was almost desperate.

"Absolutely. All of it. I understand better than you realize. Everyone loves Theo. He's kind, he's got a good heart, and he can laugh, and he can make a patient laugh the night before surgery. Not I. No, I know all too well exactly what you mean. Clarice and my late wife would tell me I was too driven, too rigid, or sometimes too austere. Maybe they were right. I was trying to protect myself from the pain by doing something."

To his surprise, Beatrix reached a hand across the table to rest it on top of his. Looking him squarely in the eyes, she said, "We both were."

"I wonder if we are still that way?" he asked.

Beatrix didn't answer.

They enjoyed their dinner and decided to walk back to the Aurora. Halfway across Mason Street, Beatrix seemed to lose her balance. "Clarice talked me into these shoes. They have heels! She said they were fashionable. I will never get used to them!" Horace took her hand and put it on his arm. This time she didn't pull away.

During their meal and conversation both of them forgot about spotting Mr. Walker coming into the restaurant. Horace paid the bill, and they left. Only then did he remember. When they got to the drugstore on the corner, Horace led Beatrix up to the plate glass window. "What are we looking at?" she asked.

"We're looking to see if Mr. Walker is anywhere behind us," he whispered. Horace pointed at something in the window while he kept scanning the reflection in the glass.

"Well, are we being followed, Horace?" Beatrix asked quietly.

"I think so. Let's stroll along slowly and find out for sure. Do you mind taking my arm again? It might make it a bit more convincing," Horace suggested.

"If you think it is essential," she said hesitantly.

They walked down a few feet to another store, peered in the window and looked at the reflection. Mr. Walker had come across the street and was now behind them. "Beatrix, why don't you go inside and look at what they've got while I sit out here on the bench?" Horace suggested.

"I do not think...oh, yes! What a good idea. Horace, I won't be long," she answered, finally taking the hint. She stepped inside, as he moved to the bench.

It didn't surprise Horace that Mr. Walker continued coming his way, slowed when he got to the bench, and spoke to him. "Nice night for a stroll, huh?" Mr. Walker asked. "Kinda glad I ran into you, Doctor Balfour. You making any progress with your investigations?"

"Oh, sometimes it takes a bit longer than you expect. We should make another jump forward before long. You?"

"Somewhat, I'd say. Well, want to keep moving," Mr. Walker replied, moving along the sidewalk. By the time Beatrix came back outside a few minutes later he was nearly out of sight.

"Now what do we do?" Beatrix asked.

"We'll go up this side to the intersection and walk back down the other side and see if he is still following us. Right now, he's about a block ahead of us, up near the park." He and Beatrix continued their window shopping, crossed Butler Street, and proceeded to slowly walk to the Butler Hotel.

"He's either following us or trying to intimidate us. It's one or the other," Horace said as they stood in front of the Post Office. "And he's beginning to intimidate me."

"This is why Saugatuck needs alleys. We could duck into a shop as if we were shopping and go out the back door," Beatrix whispered. From the sound of her voice it was obvious she was anxious for their safety.

"The only thing to do is take our time walking toward the White House, and then get back to the boat," Horace told her. "I'll ask Theo to discuss our Mr. Walker with Chief Garrison in the morning."

"That assumes nothing happens between now and then," Beatrix said. She had taken Horace's arm and was holding it tightly.

CHAPTER SEVENTEEN

"I saw the Chief," Theo told Horace and Beatrix a little after eight the next morning.

"And what did he say?" Horace asked.

"Well, I told him that we might have flushed out a suspect, your Mr. Walker, and that we might be very close to finishing our investigation," Theo said.

"And did he say that he would search for Mr. Walker?" Beatrix asked.

"Oh yes! I reminded him that if Walker confesses, he'd have solved the case," Theo smiled.

"That should work. But, I still think we need to be careful until he is apprehended," Beatrix cautioned. "I do not want that man pointing a gun at us." She paused. "Or anyone."

"So, do we have a plan?" Theo asked once they arrived at Miss Nason's house an hour later.

"We'll start at the top and work our way down," Horace replied. "Meanwhile, Fred, you're posted on guard duty out here. We saw our Mr. Walker last evening and I don't know where he may be lurking. We don't need to get jumped. Keep your eyes peeled for him."

"You can count on me! You getting yourself ambushed happened enough the last couple of years. It kinda sorta gets old," he answered. "I see him, and I'll sing out and warn you."

"And Horace, remember, I do not want another gun pointed at me ever again!" Beatrix said hotly.

"Duly noted," Horace replied.

"The attic is as good a place to start as anywhere else," Theo offered.

"Doctors, if there is anything hidden somewhere, we know it is going to be very well hidden, indeed," Beatrix reminded them as they trudged up the stairs. "It could be anywhere. It might help if we tapped on the walls for any unusual sounds."

"There is no attic," Theo reported to Beatrix. "We looked in all of the bedrooms for an opening into a crawl space. Nothing. All the ceilings are solid, plastered, and there is no sign of any way further up. Let's start on the downstairs rooms."

"I assume you checked the bathroom and closet ceilings?" Beatrix asked. Theo assured her that they had done a careful job.

They had been crawling around on their hands and knees, rubbing their fingers along the walls, prying at the mouldings where the floor met the walls, for well over an hour. They were having no luck.

"Hold on, everyone, we're looking in the wrong places. Look, the woman hoarded yarn; she devoted a whole room to it. It's where she went when she felt threatened, and where she died. If she hid something I think she must have hidden it there," Horace said. "Let's check that room, and if we don't have any luck, then we can come back up here."

"Well done, Sherlock. Hiding it in the most logical location," Beatrix smiled.

They paused at the doorway, looking into the yarn room. "All right, opposite us is an exterior wall. There would be no place to hide anything in it. And even if there were room, our secretive little Fairy Nightshade would have worried someone could pull off the siding and help themselves by coming in from the outside," Beatrix said. "We can rule out the outside wall."

"Very biblical of you, Beatrix," Theo said. "Thieves breaking in, and all that."

"Thank you. Now, that leaves three interior walls, if we count this one with the door. This is obviously not a load-bearing wall or it would be thicker. I doubt there would be room between the studs on this side, so that means one of the other two walls. If it is even the right room," she said.

"You know, when we straightened up this room, we didn't look at the wall," Horace reminded them. "Let's slide that shelving unit that we put back together and see if there is anything behind it. Carefully. We don't want a repeat of the last time it came down."

The three of them very carefully held onto the two sections and pulled them out at an angle to get a good look. "It's solid," Theo groaned. "Not a sign of anything. Not on the wall, not on the floor. Might as well put it back and try the one on the other side."

They stepped across to the other side of the room, carefully sliding out the two shelving units, one on top of the other. "Now, this might be promising," Horace said as he pointed out how the two parts had been fastened together. "Let's hope we're about to get lucky."

Beatrix gasped in surprise, pointing to the floor moulding and toe board. "Look, it's been cut! Let's push this a bit farther out of the way so we can get in there."

"Don't get your hopes up just yet. That might be nothing more than a patch or some repair work," Theo cautioned.

Horace crawled on his hands and knees, and then tugged on a section of moulding to pry it loose. He smiled as he held it up for Theo to set out of the way. "And what to my wondering eyes should appear, but a hidey hole. An old fashioned drop-hole safe."

"What's in there?" Beatrix asked. "Did we find anything?"

"I don't know yet. It looks like she cut out part of it so she could drop something down a hole," Horace said. He reached a bit deeper into the narrow space.

"Well, what's in there!" Theo demanded urgently.

Horace turned to look at him, nodded his head and said, "We found it. Bank bags! Canvas bank bags. At least, that's what it feels like." He turned around to lift one out. "And very heavy. It's not paper cash."

Horace handed the first bag to his brother. Theo struggled with the tie-cord for a few seconds, loosened it, and said, "Silver dollars. No wonder it's heavy. Does this bag have any friends in there?"

"At least one more bag." He worked it out of the hole and put it on the floor.

From inside the yarn room they heard the screen door slam shut. All three looked up in alarm, and froze in place. A few moments later Fred was in the doorway. Standing with him was the Mouse, holding a very small pistol under his right jaw. "Got jumped," he mumbled. "I wasn't expecting a woman to get the drop on me."

The Mouse let out a piercing cackle. "When I saw the four of you pulling up tp the house, I hid in the bushes, and then when I saw he was alone, I figured you three were here snooping. I gave you some time to poke around and maybe find something I want. Looks like I was right," the little woman said. She looked down at the two canvas bank bags on the floor and smiled. "I know what you're thinking – that she's holding just a Derringer – but it's still deadly. If I pull the trigger it won't be pretty. Besides, I brought along something else." She reached in her jacket pocket and pulled out a test tube with a white watery substance.

"Phosphorous?" Beatrix whispered to Horace.

"Looks like it," he answered.

"I may be an old lady, but my hearing is superb. Yes, it's phosphorous. It's easy to make and very effective. Now, enough of this jibber-jabber! Slide that bag of money over. Gently so we don't spill any of it, and don't try to do anything tricky. That belongs to me. I spent a life-time earning it. It's mine!" Her voice was hard and bitter.

"Do as she says, Horace," Theo told him.

Horace nodded, his mouth and throat dry as he slid the first bag across the floor toward where she was standing.

"That it? You'd better not be holding out on me," she snapped. "Where's that other bag you were trying to hide back behind you?"

Horace pushed it over.

"Keep looking. Maybe there's another one waiting for me," the Mouse said. "I always knew she had three bags of it hidden around here. Find it!"

"I can feel another bag," Horace said, pulling it out of the small opening. The woman motioned to slide it over in her direction, pushing the gun tighter into Fred's neck. "There is no need for this gunplay," Horace said firmly.

The Mouse snarled in derision. "You're right. All I have to do is drop this vial and the whole house goes up in flames. Ever hear of phosphorus? Course you have! You were in the war and you know what it does. Well, that's what I'm holding, and you don't want me to drop it." She laughed, sounding even more deranged. "Maybe you'd like to find out? I could throw it at you and you'll see what a good batch this is!"

"You have what you came for, now let Fred go," Horace said firmly. The Mouse ignored him.

"All right, you push those bags out to the other side of the door, one at a time, and don't try anything. Just do it nice and easy, and get it into the hall. Use your feet to do it," the Mouse told Fred, pushing the Derringer against his jaw again.

Fred did as she told him, and once the bags were in the hall, she ordered him back into the room, the gun still pressed tightly against him. "You all are going to stay right here. You open this door and you're going to smash the vial of phosphorus and you're going to burn to death right here. Just stay put. Sooner or later someone will come looking for you!" She laughed again and pushed Fred further into the room, tumbling him against the others, who tried to catch him.

The Mouse did not take careful aim. She fired a single shot into the room and closed the door. She fired a second shot into the wood for emphasis.

CHAPTER EIGHTEEN

"Thunderation, woman, I know I've been shot!" Horace bellowed, pressing the palm of his hand against the outside of his right thigh. A thin trickle of blood was already oozing between his fingers and trailing down his trousers. He panted for air, the color draining out of his face. "The bullet didn't hit the bone." He released the pressure against his leg, looking carefully to see what would happen. "Or an artery or vein. But thunderation, that woman ruined my good summer suit!" he added.

"Help me get him down on the floor," Theo ordered Fred and Beatrix. "Those shears," he said, pointing to scissors on the small table. "Hand them to me."

"That's my good suit!" Horace protested a second time as his brother opened the scissors and started cutting up the pant leg.

"Not now it isn't. Fabric's ripped and you got a blood stain on it," Theo quipped.

"This is not the time to think about that, Horace," Beatrix said. She waited for Theo to make the cut and then rip open the fabric, and took the shears from him. "And if it makes you feel any better, this is my best, well, very good petticoat. I have to take it off to make a bandage. Would you mind averting your eyes for a moment?"

The three men did, and she quickly pulled down her slip and stepped out of it. "Bandages," she said. "Nothing more than bandages!" She handed the garment to Theo to cut into strips, then got on the floor next to Horace.

Theo snipped at the fabric and ripped it into long shreds.

"Good thing you have long legs, Beatrix," Horace said as he winced in pain.

"This is not the time to be discussing my legs. But, thank you for noticing."

"I thought you once told me you didn't have any bedside manner," Horace winked at her.

"Just like the old days, doing a field dressing, right big brother?" Theo asked. "Only this time you're the patient."

"Yeah. I just hope you're a lot more gentle than we were with some of those boys," Horace panted. He flinched in pain when his brother brushed against his upper leg.

"We gotta get the boss outa here," Fred said.

"Do not open that door, Fred!" Beatrix reminded him. "She said she was..."

"I know what she said, Doc, but we can't stay here until someone comes by." He gingerly turned the knob, then told the others, "It's not locked. That's a good sign!"

Beatrix held Horace, his head on her lap, an arm around his chest to keep him from flinching. Theo began by folding up the first strip of cloth to make a bandage, then began wrapping the leg with the next strips. "I'm going to have to tie this for now, but at least it will stop the bleeding," he told his brother.

"It appears to be working," Beatrix announced. She reached down to apply pressure to the dressing.

"Alright, let's think this through," Theo said. "You two help me get Horace up on his feet and closer to the door. If that phosphorous goes up, then we have a split second to get out of here before we're goners."

They got Horace to his feet, listening to him fuss and complain. "I swear you're the worst patient in the world." Theo told his brother. "You got lucky. Better than you deserve for all the fuss you're making about a little flesh wound."

"Beatrix, if that bottle tumbles over you get out the door, and we're going to be right behind you. You'll be ahead of Horace so pull him along. We'll push from behind. Everyone clear about that? We get into the hall, all four of us, and straight out the door to the curb.

All right, Fred — go ahead, gently start opening the door, and get us out of here."

Fred dropped quietly and softly to his hands and knees, then flat on the floor, and looked through the small space between it and the bottom of the door. He could see the bottle. With a nod to Beatrix who turned the door knob, he began pushing the door open a fraction of an inch at a time. He stopped and stretched out on the floor, his head at an angle, so he could look under the door again. "Bottle's there, but she's sliding along with the door," he said quietly. "Ready?"

Theo nodded. Fred slowly opened the door a bit wider. "That there bottle is just out of reach," he fussed. He continued, inching the door open, listening carefully to make certain the glass vial was sliding along with the door.

"All right, I think I can squeeze through there," Fred whispered. "Doctor Howell, you want to hold on tight to the door so I don't bump it?"

She nodded and gripped the handle firmly. "Ready."

Slowly and carefully, Fred slipped out of the yarn room. "Got it! All safe and secure! All clear! Go ahead and come on out."

"Take that bottle outside and be careful with it!" Horace barked. "Thunderation, after all of this we don't need you having a case of the butterfingers and burning down the village. Or yourself!"

Theo looked at Beatrix, shook his head and said, "I told you he'd live." She forced a smile.

"Okay, Horace, time to get you to the hospital and patched up," Theo said urgently.

"No! Just a minute. Get me back to the Aurora!"

"The hospital would be better," Beatrix tried telling him.

"No. My boat is better. If this wound isn't all that bad, you can sew it up there. I'd rather have you do it than Landis. Second, we know the Mouse is the killer, and she is on the loose. Fred and Captain Garwood can keep her away and all of you safe.

"Get me into the car," he told them a second time. "And then scout around the grounds and see if you can find the money bags. As much as they weigh, she couldn't have gotten far with them. Get them now, or we'll never lay hold of them. It's the only chance."

With Theo and Fred on either side of him, and a very calm Beatrix holding the back seat door open, Horace was helped into the car.

"This is no time to be looking around for the money!" Beatrix snapped at Horace. "You've been shot!"

"Go take a quick look," he replied. "It may be the only chance to get it before someone else finds it. Just go and look around. A little woman like that couldn't have gotten very far with those bags. They're too heavy. She probably hid them. Try the bushes. That's where she said she was hiding when we drove up. And Beatrix, you'd better take this," he winced, turning to hand her his silver-headed walking stick.

"Horace, I've learned never to be around you without protection," she sighed and then smiled. She pulled up the hem of her skirt and showed him a small sheathed knife in a garter. "And you are repeating yourself."

"You never cease to amaze me. My guess is that if you look around, the Mouse may have dropped her pistol. You could add to your collection. Get going, would you?"

Beatrix joined Horace and Theo, looking in the bushes and under some of the shrubs for one or more of the canvas bags. She saw a flash of silver reflecting off to the side, and thinking that it might be one of the coins, went to pick it up. It wasn't a coin, and after looking around to make sure no one was watching, she pulled out her handkerchief and picked up the Mouse's Derringer.

"Theo, Fred! This way. I found her trail," Beatrix shouted.

"Got 'em, Boss!" Fred said loudly as he, Beatrix, and Theo came across the lawn, each carrying a heavy bag. "Found them under the bushes. Good thinking Boss. All three bags!"

"Probably ran out of adrenaline," Theo puffed when he got to the car.

"Who? You or the Mouse?" Horace quipped.

"I'd say she's getting increasingly unstable and dangerous," Beatrix observed quietly. "She may have had a plan, but it is collapsing on her. At least I have the gun she held on Fred! We need to get out of here. Stat!"

"That will make her more dangerous," Horace whispered, trying to catch his breath. "Let's get back to the boat. I hate to admit it, but this leg is beginning to throb."

"I have her pistol," Beatrix said.

"You have a pistol. And no telling how much more of that phosphorus she has! Let's get to the boat!"

Beatrix looked at him. His face was pale and cool. "Horace," she said calmly. "Horace, you must focus on me right now. Listen to me. I need to see your eyes looking at me. I believe you are starting to go into shock. Your face is drained of color and you feel clammy. Listen to me – this is serious. I am going to stay right here with you. Try very hard to stay awake. Stay with me!" She motioned to Fred and Theo to move a bit faster getting back to the boat.

"Do you mind if we don't go out for dinner tonight?" Horace asked quietly. "The idea of whitefish isn't very appealing right now."

"Why don't we stay in and forget all about going out for dinner or dancing," Beatrix said to him. To her relief, they were within a block of the boat.

Beatrix instantly took charge once they arrived at the Aurora. "Fred, you and Captain Garwood must stand guard. First, we get Horace into the library, and then Theo, go to the captain, and tell him to come down here. Fred, Horace's revolver is in the right top drawer of his desk. Get it, make sure it is loaded, and take a box of shells. After that, once you get the money on the boat, do not let anyone come aboard. That includes Phoebe and Harriet. Is that clear?"

Together, one on each side of him, they helped Horace limp and hop up the gangplank and across the deck. He collapsed in agony into a chair.

"Mrs. Balfour and Mrs. Garwood are in town shopping," the Captain told Beatrix when she came out on deck. "We've got to keep it down for them."

"Raise the gangplank now and lower it for them when they return, Captain," Beatrix ordered. "Fred can explain everything. Keep your eyes open for them so they can get on board in a hurry. I do not want Phoebe or her mother on the Aurora right now."

"Yes, Ma'am!" the captain said, touching a couple of fingers to his forehead.

"Fred where are those three bags?" she demanded.

"They'll be aboard in three shakes of a lamb's tail," he told her.

"Horace, how are you doing?" Beatrix asked while Theo organized the medical equipment he would need and prepared a surgical tray.

Horace gave her a pained look with a thin smile. "All right. It just stings a lot. Beatrix, there is a bottle of laudanum in my study."

"You know, you just proved the old adage that doctors make the worst patients. It is just a flesh wound, and all Theo is going to do is sew it up. The bullet barely grazed you. All across the country there are young boys who fell out of trees or slid into first base with cuts no worse than yours. There is no need to go to extremes," she said firmly. "However, two fingers of Scotch might be in order." She walked into his library to get the bottle. She paused, looked at the bottle, and pulled out the cork. Beatrix exhaled hard and took a mouthful.

"Very funny," Horace muttered at Beatrix, then winked.

"Alright, big brother, time to lose the shoes, socks, and pants," Theo said. "And Beatrix, pull the cork on that bottle for him to bite down on."

"I don't think that is necessary," Horace said.

"Really? You know, if you'd read Zane Gray instead of all those Sherlock Holmes stories, you'd know that when the town doc takes a slug out of a cowboy, he has the patient bite a cork. Right now I'm the doctor here, remember, so do as you're told!"

"Thunderation! I was talking about coming out of half my clothes!"

"She's a physician! I'm sure Doctor Howell has seen a patient's legs before!" Theo snapped at him. "And his BVDs."

"Yes, but not this patient!"

"Now. Pull down your suspenders so I can get you out of your pants. I've got work to do!" Theo turned to Beatrix and added, "Better bring another two glasses. You and I are going to need them if we have to put up with much more of his fussing." He winked, letting her know he was teasing. "Give me a hand washing the wound, would you? And you, big brother, much more of your fussing and I'm going to get out the ether and put you under. It's just a minor cut."

When Theo was ready to suture the wound, Beatrix moved back to hold Horace in case he flinched. Eighteen stitches accompanied by as many flinches, each producing a yelp of pain – and twenty-three minutes later, Theo snipped the final thread. "Done. You were a very good patient, Horace. If you were a little younger, I'd have my nurse give you a lollipop for being such a brave little man. I hope you appreciate my needlework, and stay off that leg a while."

"I think I'd rather have some of that pain medication," he told them. "And since you are so good with a needle and thread, how about sewing my trousers?"

"Horace, that may have been your best summer suit, but you've had it for decades. It's threadbare on the collar and cuffs, and the portion of the trousers are shining where the bottom meets the chair. It's a disgraceful old rag that shouldn't have been seen in public. That suit doesn't owe you a thing. Besides, Mrs. G. will never get the blood stains out. Is that your only suit?"

"No, I've got four more in my cabin."

"Four! Time to break one of them out and start wearing it!" Theo retorted. "If Clarice caught me wearing something that old she would burn. Just swallow hard and wear a different suit."

"I could, but I'm saving them for good," Horace told him.

"Have it your way, but this suit is going into the trash. And, you're going to your library and put your leg up. Beatrix, would you get a robe from his cabin?"

"I don't want to wear a robe. Bring me some proper trousers, please," he begged.

"A robe. I want to check that wound in an hour, and besides, if you move around too much you'll start bleeding again. You'll be the first man I know to ruin two suits in one day."

"There's another reason I want trousers. Sooner or later Phoebe is going to turn up, and I don't want to scare her. Trousers, Beatrix, if you please. Preferably black so it won't show the blood stains."

Beatrix had remained calm and focused ever since the Mouse appeared at the door. Suddenly, he was shaking when she stood up, and had to steady herself for a moment, then hurried from the library.

"Just the black ones in the wardrobe, not the black suit," Horace called after her.

CHAPTER NINETEEN

"How's Phoebe doing now?" Theo asked Clarice two hours later. "Seeing Horace like that was a horrible shock for her, and I don't think she took it any too well, do you?"

"I think she is still a little shaken. She cried herself out and fell asleep next to him, and he's got his arm over her shoulder. It can't be comfortable for him, but Horace won't move."

"That's Horace for you. He pretends he doesn't have a heart, but he does," Theo said softly.

"So do you. How are you doing?"

"All right now. I don't mind telling you, it scared me when I saw him get hit."

Clarice reached up and wrapped her arms around his neck, giving him a long hug. "Where's Beatrix?" she asked.

"Probably in her cabin. Packing, of all things. She said she's going back home. I don't know if she'll even say goodbye to Horace," Theo said quietly. "I feel sorry for her, but for the life of me, I can't figure that woman out."

Clarice gasped, turned on her heels and headed for Beatrix's cabin, trying to come up with a way to convince her to stay. She knocked on the door, still not knowing what she was going to say or do. Beatrix didn't answer.

She knocked again on the door, this time not waiting for an invitation as she stepped inside. "For the life of me, Beatrix, I don't know what to say other than 'please don't go.'"

Beatrix was talking to herself, "Too much chaos," over and over again, and didn't acknowledge Clarice's presence. All Clarice could do was stand helplessly in the middle of the room, fighting back tears as Beatrix meticulously folded her clothes and put them in her valise.

"I don't know what I would do if I almost lost the man I...," Clarice tried to say, then faltered. "Just please don't go. Give it some time."

Beatrix said nothing, and continued folding her clothes. Then she stood up to stretch her back. Without looking at Clarice she said, "Too much confusion. There is too much pain in the world, and now it is here. It is too much. It's all too much. I must go," she said resumed her work.

"Now what?" Clarice almost wailed when she heard a police siren out on the street.

Beatrix looked up, and Clarice pointed out the porthole. "The police chief just pulled up and I'm sure he's coming on board. Look, I know you don't want to talk about any of this now, and maybe you never will, but you must not leave until this is wrapped up."

"Perhaps," Beatrix barely whispered.

"There is no 'perhaps' about it. Your responsibility here isn't done. Help finish this murder investigation and then go, if that is what you are determined to do. Right now, Horace needs you. So, stop what you're doing, splash some water on your face, and come with me. And splash on some scent. If anyone notices your eyes, tell them you got a bit of it in them. Now, Beatrix," Clarice commanded.

"I don't use scent," she said flatly.

Clarice left Beatrix's cabin for a second and returned with a small crystal bottle and squeeze bulb. "It's only some very weak rose water," she said as she spritzed a little on Beatrix.

The chief was already in Horace's library, and Phoebe had been rather unceremoniously dismissed by Garrison. "Adult stuff, so you'd better wait outside, missy," he told her. Still wanting to be around adults she knew, she hurried off to find Mrs. Garwood in the galley.

"The chief was just saying he collared our Mr. Walker," Horace said. "Good news capturing Mr. Walker, wouldn't you say?"

"Collared him, nothing. I got the drop on him. He's in one of the cells right now. I'll give him a while to think things over, and then maybe he'll feel like talking a bit more. He ought to consider himself lucky he's not in the big city where they know how to make his type talk. They work them over pretty good in some places. Say, you were right about him being a grifter, all right. He's a regular confidence man, least wise he would be if he was any good at it. Warrants in two states besides here in Michigan."

"Well, good work Chief. Right Beatrix?" Horace said. She didn't answer. She stood with her back against a wall, silently observing.

"Yeah, well that isn't all. I've had a busy day. I got a real crazy lady out in the car. Had to cuff her wrists and ankles to keep her from lashing out. Much more of her yammering and I'm going to stick a sock in her mouth. She was shouting and screaming that she killed Fairy Nightshade and that she shot you! Can you beat it? I figure she went right round the bend after her friend died. I tell you, she's a real loony, really spiffilated, and if she keeps this up, she's going to get a one-way ride to the loony bin!" The chief gloated. Then he stopped and asked seriously, and "Did that woman shoot you?"

"Chief, do I look like I've been shot? No, wait a minute. I think I had a shot or two of that Scotch. Prescribed by a physician. I'll prescribe one for you, if you think you need something to relax," Horace offered. "Is this woman who claims she shot me the same one people keep calling the Mouse? No one has seen her around town since Decoration Day."

"Yeah, the one and only Little Miss Mouse. Quiet as a mouse most of the time, only I think she went lulu and she's kicking up a ruckus. I figure maybe Doc Landis can give her a shot of something to calm her down."

"I believe, Chief, that if you would allow us to examine her, talk to her, that is, we might be of some help," Beatrix said slowly and carefully. When Horace looked at her, she ran her finger across the right side of her nose. Her smile was missing. He could tell something was very wrong.

"Doctor Howell might be right," he said. "We'd be happy to help."

"Yeah, I figure I owe you one, seeing as how you put the finger on that grifter. Sure, why not? My deputy and I'll bring her up here," the chief smiled. "She's all yours. I got plenty of work to do without having to handle a nut-case. She's small enough he can throw her over his shoulder like a bag of spuds and carry her in."

"This may take a while, chief. Why don't you have your deputy stay here so you can get on with your other work? It'll give you a chance to do your reports without interference. Mrs. Garwood usually has some pie or cake cooling by about this time of day. She'll give your man something to eat while he waits. And, you might enjoy a little break to sort things out," Horace suggested.

The chief agreed, posting his deputy just outside the door of the library to make sure the Mouse didn't escape.

"I understand you're claiming you killed Miss Nason," Horace said, looking at the woman when she was put on a chair. She began to calm down.

"I didn't mean to shoot you! I only wanted to scare you," she said quickly.

"Well, you did shoot me," Horace said firmly. "You could have killed any of us."

"I said I didn't mean to shoot you," she retorted.

"But you did kill Miss Nason, did you not?" Beatrix asked.

"Yes! Yes I did, and I'm glad I did it. She deserved it! My sister was a wicked woman who hurt everyone! I'm glad she's dead!"

Beatrix interrupted, her eyes wide, "You said, your sister? How very interesting. Miss Nason was your sister?"

The Mouse stared at Beatrix, then unleashed a torrent of words. "Yes. We aren't blood sisters. My parents didn't think they could have children and they made arrangements to adopt me from an orphan train when it came through. Only by then, Mother was in the family way – with that woman. Our folks did all right by us, raised us up the same as if I was their own, but then one day when I was about eight or so, Phyllis found out I was adopted. She said she found out when she was snooping through Papa's desk and found the papers. That's how she found out. At first, she just teased me about it and called me all sorts of names. After that she made my life hell on earth. It's been that way for years. Ever since I was eight! Do you hear me? Since I was eight!" She settled back to continue.

"Our folks gave us some pocket money, an allowance. It wasn't much, but it was our money. It was my money, but she said if I didn't give her half of it that she'd tell everyone in school I was an adopted little bastard. I should have let her do it. I could have stopped her right from the start, but I was scared of her. I've always been scared of her. Scared of what the others would say. The shame would be nothing compared to the rest of my life. She loved hurting people and blackmailing them. She got money from me, and then she did it to one of the teachers! A teacher! All because she saw her walking out with another teacher. She told her that if she didn't pay her to keep quiet, she was going to get her fired.

"Little miss goody two-shoes one moment and Satan herself the next."

"That must have been horrible," Beatrix said quietly.

"It got worse and worse. When I was a senior in school, Phyllis said she'd see to it no man would ever want me!" In a flash she opened her blouse and partially pushed down her camisole. "Take a look at those scars! She did that to me with a knife!" she wailed. Both Beatrix and Horace gasped in horror. "She said if I told, she'd tell them I did it to myself.

"She treated me like her slave. You heard about all those awards she won for her knitting? She didn't do a single stitch. I did it. She made me. I did the work for her, and she would never let me enter so much as a lousy county fair in case I might get a ribbon or a quarter dollar cash prize. My knitting. It was my knitting! And all the time running around snooping on people and finding out their secrets and then making them pay to keep her quiet!

"I thought I had escaped her by moving up here to teach. I didn't tell anyone where I went. Not a single friend, but then she found out and she moved up here, and she laughed about how nothing would ever change. People here had money, lots of money, and she wanted it. I saw how she hurt people up here, the same way she did all her life. She knew all their secrets and made up wild stories that would destroy them."

"And on Decoration Day, what happened, Bertha?" Horace asked. "The day you killed her?"

"We were getting ready for the parade, and I saw her talking to the commander. He's a good man, a real American Army hero during the war, and he was proud of it. Did you see his medals? Well, he earned them, but she told him if he didn't pay her money, she was going to start a rumor that he bought them. Bought them! He earned them! In combat! It just wasn't right. And then she came up to you, Doctor Balfour, and she was about to start on you when your granddaughter interrupted you. So I went up to her, right up to her and told her to her face that it was over, that she was finished hurting people. I couldn't take it anymore. I had to make it stop so I went over to her house and took this box she had full of ribbons. All those years of ribbons I earned, and she was so proud of them.

"I put them into her cast iron skillet to burn them. I knew she had money in the house and I didn't want it to burn down, so I was careful. I knew what I was doing. That's why I used the skillet. I wanted to destroy something that belonged to her, like she destroyed everything that should have been mine!"

"Where did you get the red phosphorus, Bertha?" Beatrix asked.

She giggled, then cackled. "You figured that out did you? Good for you. You're a smart woman. Well, I'll tell you how I got it. One of my students went over there in the war, and he told me how they made it when they couldn't get the real stuff, and used it with trip wires in No Man's Land. If a German tripped the wire there'd be a big explosion. He wrote and told me how they made it, and I made some of it for myself. I was going to burn her house down with her in it years ago, and I had the stuff all this time, only it had gone bad. It had to be heated up...."

"How did you get there ahead of her? We saw she had a bicycle," Theo said.

The Mouse snorted. "Her bike was down the next block, padlocked to a street lamp. She had to go back to get it, and my bicycle was close. I got there ahead of her!" She roared with laughter, imagining her sister hurrying back to get her bicycle. "No one ever notices the Mouse!"

"So you put it and her ribbons in the cast iron skillet and turned on the gas? Is that it?" Horace asked.

Phyllis cackled maniacally again. "She came in the front door and saw me doing it. She screamed and screamed at me, and then maybe she didn't believe that her little mouse would do it. And then the phosphorous caught fire, just as she was watching. She saw it all! Revenge for a lifetime of hurting people! She went into the yarn room to look for her box where she kept it on the top shelf, just to see for herself. And I pushed the shelves down on top of her. I didn't mean to kill her, but I killed her, and I'm happy I did. She deserved to die!"

"And the money?" Beatrix asked. "Do you think you deserve it?"

Phyllis looked at her and calmly said, "Yes. After a lifetime of her, I deserve every cent of it and ten times more! And you all deserved to die because you tried to keep me from it! I should have thrown that bottle of phosphorus at the door and let you burn up with the rest of the house!"

Horace stood up and limped awkwardly to the door and opened it. "Constable, I think Miss Lee is ready to leave. At least we are certainly ready for her to leave us."

"Ah, I don't have the squad car. The chief took it with him."

Horace offered to have Fred drive the two of them back to the station.

"By the way, Fred, just what did you do with that vial of phosphorus?" Beatrix asked.

"Oh, say, it's a good thing you reminded me about that stuff! I kinda sorta forgot I've still got it right here in my coat pocket. I guess I kinda sorta forgot about it in all the excitement!" He reached in his pocket and gave it to his boss.

"Take this and throw it into the river! It's the only safe thing to do! Throw it far out into the river, and don't hit any boats." Horace said as he handed it back to him.

"I believe, Horace, you need to sit down and put your leg up. You are quite ashen and it has been an exhausting day," Beatrix said. "Take my arm to steady yourself." She helped him to his leather chair.

CHAPTER TWENTY

"Where's Theo?" Horace asked as he slumped back in his leather chair. Beatrix said she would find him and bring him to the office, cautioning Horace not to move around while she was gone. She returned a few minutes later with Theo, and said she would leave them alone. "I have some things I am doing," she said quietly. Her voice was distant, and she was repeating herself, obviously distracted by something troubling her.

"I'd rather you'd stay. We could use your brains on this," Horace said. For the next few minutes they reviewed the recent conversations with the police chief and the Mouse. Even though they had solved the murder, or at least brought it to a conclusion, none of them felt very cheerful.

"Well, I'd say that's done then," Theo said. "She'll be arrested, and charged with murder, and since she confessed, she'll probably spend the rest of her life in prison. At her age, at least it won't be for decades. That's something, I suppose. It's too bad. Sad, really, in some ways."

"Yeah, it is," Horace sighed. "Sad in every way, all-around."

"I believe there are some better possibilities," Beatrix said softly, her head down. "She is..." her voice trailed off, "...in terrible pain."

"What do you have in mind?" Horace asked.

"She is troubled. Her entire life has been constant pain. I think she should be institutionalized, not imprisoned," she said distantly, her mind obviously whirling with ideas.

"She tried killing us, remember?" Theo told her.

"I know, and when we talked with her, it was not the doings of a sane woman; not a sane person, man or woman. She had a lifetime of abuse that made her the way she is. You saw the scars on her breasts. Her sister did that to her to ruin her hopes for love or intimacy. I believe she saw killing her sister and as the only way to stop the pain. There is so much pain for so many people in all of this," Beatrix said firmly. She got up and left the library, returning to her cabin.

"Beatrix might be onto something. I hadn't thought of the psychological side of it," Theo said. "Surprising to hear it from Beatrix."

"More than just the psychological side. The human side. Beatrix has a good heart and a sharp mind," Horace replied. "You're right, she might be onto something. Maybe there is something we can do besides sending her off to spend the rest of her life in prison." He pulled out his pipe and slowly filled it. "There's got to be something better."

"If you figure it out, let me know. You should get some rest, too. Want me to pour you something to help cut the pain a bit?"

"No. Not now. I'll let you know if I come up with an idea."

"I'm glad you're here," Horace said an hour later when Beatrix came to check on him. She had quietly tapped on the door, not wanting to wake him if he had drifted off to sleep. He was awake, re-lighting his pipe, and there was already a thick cloud of smoke in the library. "I have an idea, and I could use your help. Poke holes in it and then we'll try again."

"Horace, I...." Beatrix started before he interrupted her, waving her to a chair.

He continued to talk. "Miss Lee is going to be charged with at least the attempted murder, if not the murder of her sister. That means there will be a trial, and no doubt she'll be sent off to prison. You said something that caught my attention – institutionalizing her. I've been thinking about it."

"Yes, that would be better," Beatrix replied. "But Horace, those state hospitals are horrible. She'll be thrown in with all sorts of people. Some of them are very dangerous. She might not live very long. Even the better ones are nothing but warehouses for people. Some of them are worse than the county poorhouses."

"I agree. But perhaps there is a private asylum...."

"I'm sure there are, but they cost a lot of money."

"I'm not concerned about the money."

"She might be there for years. What if she outlives you? Then what happens to her? Turned loose? Sent to prison? Maybe end up in the poor house?"

"But you agree it would be the best solution for her, don't you?"

"Yes, so far, at least," she said distantly.

"Well, if Landis examines her and would be willing to sign the papers that she is certifiable, then we can go from there."

"Yes," she said slowly and cautiously. "It would still require a judge to sign the committal papers, and then there is the problem of finding an asylum and paying for it."

"I know you fly a plane. Can you drive a car?" he asked brightly.

"Horace, I was in the midst of something," she tried telling him a second time.

"This won't take more than a few minutes. Drive us over to the hospital and we'll see Landis. I'd drive myself, but ...." he pointed to his leg.

Beatrix winced but agreed.

"You didn't answer about whether you know how to drive."

"Yes, Horace, I know how to drive, and I have an automobile of my own. Two, in fact. I still have my mother's Edison Electric, and just this year I bought a new two-seater Hupmobile."

Horace shook his head in disbelief. "An electric and a Hup? You never cease to amaze me. Let's go and have a chin wag with the town doc."

"On one condition. You stay in the car and I'll ask Doctor Landis to come out to see you."

"Us," he corrected her. "I need your help."

"Us," she reluctantly repeated.

"It's a creative idea," Landis said after hearing out Horace and Beatrix. "And, completely plausible. Yeah, it just might work. She gets charged for murder, and there is a trial. I think we know the probable outcome. She'll be found guilty and sent to prison. But if she's certified, and if the judge agrees, we can have her committed right away and avoid a trial. The only challenge is to get the county prosecutor and judge to agree."

"By any chance do you know them well enough to ask them to make this happen?" Horace asked.

"Yeah," Landis said slowly, still thinking over the plan. "Basically, it's a gentleman's agreement with the prosecutor, and then the judge will agree to it and sign the committal papers."

"And if you certified her, how long would it take?" Horace asked.

"Oh, it's probably something that could be wrapped up in a couple of hours. Then comes the challenge of finding a place for her to go," Landis said.

"Do you have any ideas?" Beatrix asked.

"As a matter of fact, I do. There's one up near Ludington that is top-drawer. They've been pestering me for the past month or so to come up and be their physician. I'd take it in a heartbeat but I can't afford to buy into the practice," Landis said wistfully.

"Buy into the practice?" Horace asked.

"It's a private institution, not a county or state facility."

Horace's face lit up with a smile.

"So, it would work?" Beatrix asked.

"Yes. Yes, it would. But you know, Chief Garrison is going to have a fit if we do it," Landis cautioned them.

"I doubt it. He's got another suspect already behind bars – a grifter who used the name Wilbur Walker around here. That should keep the Chief busy for a few days," Horace said, smiling.

"People might say that you're railroading her off to a nut house. Let's face it, people talk," Landis cautioned.

"I doubt they will, this time," Beatrix said.

"I agree with her," Horace added. "See what you can do, would you? The sooner the better."

"You are nowhere close to being finished with this," Beatrix reminded Horace after she helped him back into his chair in the library.

"I know," he winced.

"There is the money, and the attempted murder," Beatrix told him.

"The only evidence Garrison has is unlawful discharge of a firearm within the village boundary, and her attempted murder when she shot me. And that would more likely be reduced to unintentional attempted homicide," Horace said, lighting his pipe, rather pleased with himself.

"What about the murder of her sister?" Beatrix demanded.

"What murder? On Decoration Day you heard the chief say that he thought Fairy Nightshade reached too high up on the shelf and accidently pulled it down on top of her. Unfortunate accident. And as for the kitchen fire, well, she put something on the stove and went into the yarn room where she died. So, on the one side is the chief's simple explanation and on the other is the Mouse with this wild story. Besides, if Landis can find a judge to sign the papers, it's over."

"Horace, you are playing fast and loose with the truth. So tell me, how are you going to explain all that money? The cash and those three bags of silver coins?"

"I'm not. Fairy Nightshade ruined her sister's life; now she's going to pay for her care. And with Landis watching over things, she will be well cared for. If we're lucky, all that leftover yarn will go with her and she will spend her last years teaching others to knit. When she's ready for that. If she is ever ready. That's up to the staff," Horace answered.

"It is a brilliant plan, I will willingly admit that, except for one thing. Landis hasn't agreed to join the practice. He said he could not afford to buy in."

"Leave that to me, Beatrix. I'll see you at dinner," Horace said. "And Beatrix, thank you."

"For what? Driving you over to Landis' office? That was very little."

"No, thank you for being here. You see, I...."

She interrupted him. "I must get back to what I was doing." She hurried out the door and returned to her cabin. Horace was anxious, knowing she was distraught.

Clarice gave Beatrix a minute, before following her to her cabin. "Still planning to leave? I wish you wouldn't?"

"I do not belong here," she sniffled. "I thought I did, but I do not. I do not fit in."

"Yes, I understand. I felt the same way when I married Theo. I thought I had married him, not his entire family and their medical practice. For the first couple of years I thought about running away. I know what you're going through, and it hurts, doesn't it?"

"Thank you for trying. It is not the same. I have to go, that is all," she said firmly. "There is too much pain. Too many people are in pain. I have been part of their pain."

"I understand. And maybe you'll think that Theo, or Phoebe, or Harriet will even be relieved, but you are wrong. That's because it will break Horace's heart."

Beatrix looked at Clarice. "People like Horace and me do not have hearts," she said flatly.

"Oh, I think that's where you are wrong, very, very wrong. You do. Beatrix, you and Horace are different. I can't put my finger on it, but you are. You two were always the loneliest children when we were youngsters. You both sat on the sidelines for everything, and then threw yourself into your work. It's too bad you couldn't at least have been lonely together, instead of you both hiding behind a book. Well, the world has benefited from what you two have done in medicine, but it's come at a terrible personal cost. You're both still lonely little children in elementary school."

Beatrix stood and looked at her.

"For a woman who doesn't have a heart, you've certainly gone out of your way just today to care for that poor deranged woman. You've taken care of Horace ever since he got shot. And I'll tell you something, Beatrix, that wasn't easy for you. I know that more than you realize. Please don't go. And if you really must, then at least say goodbye to Horace. Too many people have vanished from his life. If you do it, it will destroy him."

Clarice turned and left Beatrix's cabin, quietly pulling the door behind her.

"What's going on?" Theo asked when Clarice came back up on deck.

"She's running away," she whispered to her husband.

The news stunned him. "What?"

"She's running away. She kept saying she doesn't fit in, doesn't belong here," Clarice said as she dabbed her handkerchief against her eyes. "We have to do something, and fast."

"Does Horace know?" Theo asked.

"I doubt it," she said quietly.

"Horace, time to listen to your little brother," Theo began. "What you don't know is that Beatrix is down in her cabin packing her grip. She's planning on taking a powder."

"What? Why?"

"Probably because you've kept her dangling on a string for the past few years. You treat her like she's your sister."

"We don't have a sister," Horace answered. Confused for a moment, he missed Theo's meaning.

"Fine. And she certainly is not your sister. She's a woman, and you can't see past her brains and your playing at Sherlock Holmes and Irene Adler. You, you, you, well, you're clueless that she's a woman who is, well, wants to be, more than a medical colleague. You're kind to her, polite, respectful, but it takes more. Have you ever kissed her good night, even a peck on the cheek? Ever walked hand in hand?"

"Well, she helped me walk after I got shot. And the night before, she took my arm walking home."

"That's what a nurse does. An orderly. If that's all she is to you – a colleague or a nurse, then by all means let her go. Convince her she's doing the right thing, that you don't care. Or do you care?" he thundered at him.

"Well, yes," Horace said quietly.

"Then you'd better do something fast or she's going to fly out of your life once and for all."

"You don't even like her!" Horace shot back.

"I don't have to like her, but you're my brother and I want you to be happy. You hear that? It's about you being happy for a change."

Horace struggled to his feet, and reached for his silver-headed walking stick, then slowly made his way, one step at a time, down to the lower deck, walking to Beatrix's room.

"I know it's a bit late for this...." he barely whispered.

"For?"

"Well, I've been thinking about it for some time, trying to work up the courage to ask you something."

"Yes?" she asked.

"Phoebs tells me that there is a mid-summer dance party at the Big Pavilion in a couple of weeks. She said a fellow named Bunk Johnson is bringing his band up. Now, I've never heard of him, but I was thinking that, well, if my leg heals up enough that is, we could go to it together. Just the two of us. I mean, if the rest of them are going, well, that's fine. They can meet up with us there. But dinner, somewhere nice, maybe at a supper club out along the lake, just the two of us. That is, if you don't mind driving. I'd like do it up right with you and me going out for dinner and then the dance. That is, if you'd like to do it, too."

She caught her breath and looked away from him. "Yes," she said quietly. "That would be very nice."

He smiled. "Good, I'm truly happy you agreed," he told her. The moment was awkward for both of them, and he moved toward the cabin door, uncertain what to say or do. "Well, if I'm going to be in shape to cut a rug with you, I'd better get off this leg."

"Horace," she said, stopping him before he left. "Please have Fred get rid of that science experiment in the engine room, and give some thought to how we get rid of those hideous boxes of diaries."

"Yes, good idea," he answered.

"And Horace, thank you for – well, thank you."

— *to be continued in*
A MURDER ON THE
SAUGATUCK CHAIN FERRY

Made in the USA
Monee, IL
01 June 2023

34705103R00108